Just a nightmare?

Jessica was falling backward. Her hands were clawing at the air. Her heart was pounding so hard, she was sure it was going to burst. She could feel the heavy ruby necklace, cold against the bare skin of her throat.

Above her loomed black storm clouds, racing across the sky. Lightning tore through the darkness. Somehow she managed to twist her head around to catch a glimpse of the earth below. In a flash of lightning, she saw rocks rushing up to meet her. Sharp, deadly rocks in a swirling black sea.

Jessica screamed.

Bantam Skylark Books in the SWEET VALLEY TWINS AND FRIENDS series.
Ask your bookseller for the books you have missed.

Sweet Valley Twins and Friends Super Editions

Sweet Valley Twins and Friends Super Chiller Editions

Sweet Valley Twins and Friends Magna Edition
THE MAGIC CHRISTMAS

SWEET VALLEY TWINS
AND FRIENDS
◇ SUPER CHILLER ◇

The Curse of the Ruby Necklace

◇

Written by
Jamie Suzanne

Created by
FRANCINE PASCAL

A BANTAM SKYLARK BOOK ®
NEW YORK • TORONTO • LONDON • SYDNEY • AUCKLAND

RL 4, 008-012

THE CURSE OF THE RUBY NECKLACE
A Bantam Skylark Book / June 1993

*Sweet Valley High® and Sweet Valley Twins and Friends® are
registered trademarks of Francine Pascal*

Conceived by Francine Pascal

*Produced by Daniel Weiss Associates, Inc.
33 West 17th Street
New York, NY 10011*

Cover art by James Mathewuse

*Skylark Books is a registered trademark of Bantam Books, a division of
Bantam Doubleday Dell Publishing Group, Inc.
Registered in U.S. Patent and Trademark Office and elsewhere.*

ISBN: 0-553-15949-6

Published simultaneously in the United States and Canada

*Bantam Books are published by Bantam Books, a division of Bantam
Doubleday Dell Publishing Group, Inc. Its trademark, consisting of the
words "Bantam Books" and the portrayal of a rooster, is Registered in
U.S. Patent and Trademark Office and in other countries. Marca
Registrada. Bantam Books, 1540 Broadway, New York, New York 10036.*

PRINTED IN THE UNITED STATES OF AMERICA

OPM   0 9 8 7 6 5 4 3 2 1

To Daniel Meir Goldstein

One

◇

"Jessica, look out behind you!" Elizabeth Wakefield shouted.

"Give me a break, Elizabeth. How dumb do you think I am?" Jessica Wakefield said, pouncing on the shiny object she'd spotted in the sand. "If I turn around to look, you'll grab it. And I saw it first, so it's mine."

"Just don't say I didn't warn you," Elizabeth called over her shoulder as she dashed away up the beach.

Jessica heard a roaring sound behind her. "Oh no!" she cried, just before a huge wave crashed over her. After a few long seconds the wave receded. Jessica spit out a mouthful of saltwater and shook her head to clear the water out of her eyes. The first thing she saw was Elizabeth, sitting on the dry sand, laughing so hard she had tears in her eyes.

"It's not funny," Jessica muttered, wringing out her hair.

"Yes, it was," Elizabeth said, trying to catch her breath. "If you hadn't been so worried about grabbing that shell, you'd still be dry."

Jessica stared at the object in her hand. It was a chain of some kind, encrusted in sand and dirt. "This isn't a shell," she said. She scraped away some of the dirt with her fingernail to reveal a shiny spot of red. It caught the afternoon sun and glittered brightly.

"What is it, then?" Elizabeth asked.

"I'm not sure," Jessica murmured, studying it intently. "A necklace, maybe."

"Can I see?"

Jessica thrust the chain into her pocket. For some reason she couldn't quite explain, she didn't want to share her discovery with Elizabeth just yet. "There's nothing to see," she said quickly. "It's covered with barnacles and dirt."

"Come on, Jess," Elizabeth said. "Let me see it."

"I said *no*, Elizabeth," Jessica snapped, surprised by her own tone of voice.

"All right, all right. You don't have to bite my head off," Elizabeth said. She pointed to the horizon, where a low bank of dark clouds was gathering. "We probably should start heading for home. It looks as though those clouds are coming our way." She frowned at Jessica. "Besides, you're obviously in a bad mood all of a sudden."

"I am *not* in a bad mood," Jessica replied irritably. They couldn't go home—not yet. Jessica still had something very important to do. She gazed out over the ocean. The clouds were miles away. Leave it to her twin to decide it was going to rain when the sun was still shining. Elizabeth could always find something to worry about.

Sometimes it was difficult for Jessica to believe that she and Elizabeth were identical twins, even though they looked exactly alike. They both had long blond hair, blue-green eyes, and dimples in their left cheeks.

But it often seemed that *all* the two girls had in common was their looks. Jessica liked to have fun and try new things—especially new clothes and makeup. She was a member of the Unicorn Club, a group of the prettiest and most popular girls at Sweet Valley Middle School. The Unicorns spent most of their spare time shopping and talking about boys.

Elizabeth, on the other hand, spent most of her time reading mysteries and writing for the *Sweet Valley Sixers*, the sixth-grade newspaper she and her friends had started. She couldn't imagine anything more boring than sitting around and gossiping with the Unicorns.

But in spite of their differences, the twins were the best of friends. They shared everything with each other, from their clothes to their deepest secrets. And no matter how much they argued sometimes, they always made up in the end.

"Look," Jessica said, "I'm sorry if I sounded grouchy about the necklace, Lizzie."

"That's OK," Elizabeth said with a smile. "You're just mad because I found all the good shells."

"Let's keep walking a little farther," Jessica suggested casually. "It's not going to rain for a while."

"But we're almost to the end of the beach," Elizabeth said. "The only thing up there is the Keller mansion."

"The Keller mansion?" Jessica echoed, trying to keep her voice neutral.

"The last time we walked past there, you said it gave you the creeps."

"That was a long time ago, Elizabeth. We were just kids." Jessica waved her hand dismissively.

"It was about two months ago," Elizabeth said. Suddenly she stopped and put her hands on her hips. "Wait a minute. You're up to something."

"Me?" Jessica did her best to look innocent. "What could I possibly be up to?"

"I'm not sure," Elizabeth replied. "But it's definitely something. First you wanted to go for a walk on the beach and look for shells—something you've never wanted to do in your entire life. And now you want to keep walking, even though it means going near the Keller mansion."

"It must be terrible always to be so suspicious, Elizabeth."

"Just tell me what you're up to," Elizabeth said, crossing her arms over her chest.

"Fine," Jessica said, pretending to pout. "Go ahead and be mad because I wanted to take you to the mansion for some excitement."

"Since when is a dusty old abandoned house exciting?"

Jessica grinned. "Since I found out a movie's being made there."

"No way."

"Way." Jessica nodded triumphantly. "And I heard they might want to hire some people to work as extras."

"Extra what?"

"*Extras*," Jessica repeated in an exasperated tone. "If you ever read any movie magazines, you'd know that an *extra* is one of those people you see in a movie who's not really a regular actor. You know—the people you see in the backround walking down the street or sitting in a restaurant."

"So *that* explains your strange behavior."

Jessica shrugged. "You know me too well."

Elizabeth laughed. "Do you really think you're going to be in a movie?"

"Why not?" Jessica tossed back her wet hair. "I have star quality."

"Mom and Dad may not think so."

"See? That's why I didn't tell you where we

were going. I knew you'd say something like that."
Jessica tilted her chin. "If you want to make it in
Hollywood, you can't let these little details get in
your way."

"I'd say Mom and Dad are a couple of pretty big
details," Elizabeth replied. "Besides, I'm not so sure
I'd want to be an extra."

"You *do* want to be a writer, though, don't you?"

"Yeah. Why?"

Jessica shrugged, trying to look nonchalant. "It
just seems to me that a story about a movie being
made right here in Sweet Valley would be great for
the *Sixers*. Of course, if you don't want to go with
me—"

Elizabeth hesitated for a second. Then she
laughed. "You know me too well, too," she said as
she fell into step beside her sister. "How did you
find out about this, anyway?"

"Well, I happened to be in the office this afternoon—"

"You got called to the principal's office again?"

"Mr. Seigel *claims* I was late to science class,"
Jessica said. "But it all worked out for the best, because while I was there I overheard Mrs. Knight
telling someone all about it on the phone." She
grinned. "With spring break coming up, I bet
everyone will want to get in on the act as soon as
they hear about it."

"What's this movie supposed to be about?"

"I don't know, but it's called *Dead Little Rich Girl*."

"Doesn't exactly sound like a comedy, does it?"

Jessica reached into her pocket and felt for the chain again. "No," she said distractedly, "it doesn't."

Just then a dark cloud blotted out the sun, and Jessica felt a shiver go up her spine. For an instant she felt terribly afraid—of what, she wasn't quite sure.

"Jess?" Elizabeth touched her on the arm. "Are you OK?"

Jessica took a deep breath and tried to shake off the dark, ominous feeling that had came over her. *It's nothing,* she told herself. *I'm just feeling a little nervous about the storm.*

"Sure I'm OK," she said. "Why wouldn't I be?" She forced a smile. "After all, I'm about to become a movie star!"

"It almost looks like a castle, doesn't it?" Elizabeth commented as the girls climbed carefully over a jumble of sharp rocks. They paused at the foot of a long stone stairway cut out of the side of the cliff, which led from the beach to the entrance of the mansion.

"It doesn't look as creepy as it did the last time we saw it," Jessica said.

Elizabeth nodded. The Keller place had always looked like the kind of house that ought to be haunted, although no one had ever gotten close enough to find out for sure. For as long as Elizabeth could remember, all the windows had been covered with boards, and a tall fence had protected it from trespassers.

But all that was changing. Some workmen were applying a new coat of white paint to the exterior. Others were removing the boards from the windows and installing new panes of glass.

"What are we waiting for?" Jessica said, starting up the stairs.

"Jessica," Elizabeth said gently, "you can't just walk in the door and expect someone to say, 'Hey, do you want to be in a movie?'"

But Jessica ignored her and kept climbing. Elizabeth glanced up at the ominous sky. With a sigh, she followed her twin up the stairs.

"Hey, great. The gate's unlocked," Jessica said when they reached the top.

Elizabeth and Jessica went through the gate and paused at the edge of the wide lawn surrounding the mansion. People were scurrying about purposefully, shouting directions to one another.

"I don't see any movie stars," Jessica said, sounding disappointed.

"Me neither," Elizabeth said. "But I have a feeling they're here." She pointed across the grounds. "See those trailers? Look on the door of that closest one. There's a name on the door in gold letters."

Jessica squinted. "S-H-A-W-N-B-R-O . . . *Shawn Brockaway!*"

"Wasn't she the girl who used to star on that really stupid TV show?"

"*Castaway Kids*," Jessica said excitedly. "Everybody knows Shawn Brockaway. She's in all the magazines, and on all the interview shows, and she was even in a music video once. She's a huge star."

"Look. Do you think those are movie people?" Elizabeth said as a man and a woman walked by. They were dressed in shorts and T-shirts and were poring over a big sheaf of papers.

Jessica wrinkled her nose. "I doubt it. Movie people are always very fashionable. I mean, that woman's wearing a baseball cap."

Suddenly the woman stopped and stared at them. "Twins!" she cried. "Look, Murray, identical twins, and just the right age!" She rushed toward them. "Hey, you two," she called.

"Yes?" Elizabeth answered, a little startled. Hadn't the woman ever seen twins before?

"How old are you?" the woman demanded.

"We're in sixth grade," Jessica volunteered.

The woman glanced over her shoulder. "How old is that, Murray?"

"Perfect," Murray said. "Lillian had just turned twelve, so these two would be perfect."

The woman put her hands on her hips and looked them up and down. "So, kids," she said, "you want to be in a movie?"

Jessica gave Elizabeth an I-told-you-so grin. Then she turned to the woman. "I think I'm free," she said casually.

"It has to be both of you. I mean, we're looking for twins," the woman said.

"Why?" Jessica asked, looking a little disappointed. "Is the movie about twins?"

"No, no, no." The woman pulled a piece of gum from the pocket of her shorts, unwrapped it, and popped it in her mouth. "Look, my name is Becka Silver. I'm the director of this movie."

"*You're* the director?" Jessica asked, looking doubtful.

"I know—you were expecting a man, right?" Becka rolled her eyes. "Well, he's me. You remember *A Fine, Drizzly Dawn*? Or *Grandpa's Ghost*? I directed both those movies."

"You directed *A Fine, Drizzly Dawn*?" Elizabeth asked in amazement. "That was a great movie!"

"The kid's got good taste," Becka remarked to Murray. "What did you think of *Grandpa's Ghost*?" she asked Elizabeth.

"Well . . ." Elizabeth didn't want to hurt Becka's feelings, but the truth was, she hadn't liked *Grandpa's Ghost* at all.

"You didn't like it, right?"

Elizabeth felt Jessica's elbow digging into her side.

"She loved it," Jessica cried enthusiastically. "I did too."

"Actually," Elizabeth said, rubbing her side, "I didn't really like it all that much."

"See, Murray?" Becka grinned. "I told you the

kid has taste. She's right. That movie was a turkey."

"So what is this about twins?" Jessica pressed.

"We like to work with twins as much as possible for the kid roles," Becka explained. "The law says that if you're a kid you can only work a certain number of hours a day, see? So if we need to keep working and we've got twins, we can just trade them off. When twin number one has worked as long as she's allowed, we bring in twin number two. You girls would be extras."

"Oh," Jessica said. She looked a little deflated.

"Hey, you have to start somewhere, right? Besides, the job pays pretty well. Probably a lot more than your allowance."

"I'll do it, but only on one condition," Elizabeth said. "I write for our class paper, and if I could do an interview—"

"Great! She's an *extra* and already she's making demands!" Becka threw up her hands. "OK, kid, you want an interview, you got it. Be here Wednesday afternoon. We'll need written permission from your parents, of course."

"Is Shawn Brockaway going to be in this movie?" Jessica asked excitedly.

Becka's shoulders slumped, and her lip seemed to curl just a bit. "Yes, heaven help us, she is." Then, without a another word, she hurried off with Murray

Two

"I can't believe it," Elizabeth marveled as she and Jessica climbed back down the long stairway to the beach. "She just walked over and offered you a job!"

"She offered *us* a job," Jessica pointed out. "We're going to be stars."

"Actually, we're going to be extras."

Jessica shrugged. She wasn't in the mood to argue with Elizabeth. In fact, she was in a very strange mood. She should have been thrilled about being in the movie, and she was, sort of, but she couldn't seem to concentrate on it.

She reached into her pocket and felt the rough surface of the necklace she'd found. Suddenly she stopped in her tracks. Without knowing why, she turned toward the mansion. Her eyes were drawn to a small balcony that jutted out over the rocky shore. The tide was in, and the surf churned wildly as it slammed into the rocks beneath the balcony.

It's a long way down to those rocks, Jessica thought. A strange chill went through her.

"What are you looking at?" Elizabeth asked. "It's going to start pouring any second."

"That balcony . . ." Jessica whispered.

"What about it?"

"I don't know. Look at it. Doesn't it make you nervous?"

Elizabeth rolled her eyes toward the threatening sky. *"You're* the one who's making me nervous. If we don't run for it, we're going to be caught in the middle of a lightning storm. And personally, I don't feel like being zapped to a crisp."

Jessica tore her eyes from the balcony. Elizabeth was right. Thunder was already rumbling in the distance, and they still had a long walk ahead of them.

As Elizabeth turned and hurried down the beach along the water's edge, Jessica trudged along behind her. She'd only gone a few yards when she paused, suddenly overcome with the desire to see the necklace again. She pulled it out of her pocket and started chipping away more of the dirt as she walked. Soon she'd revealed a smooth red stone, almost pretty enough to be a real jewel. Just then a big drop of rain landed right on her head.

"Great," Elizabeth complained. "We're going to

get soaked." More drops fell, dotting the sand. "Hurry, Jess!"

A moment later the clouds opened up and rain began to fall by the bucketful, drenching the twins as they ran. A jagged bolt of lightning tore through the clouds. Jessica jumped at the deafening crack of thunder that followed, and the necklace fell from her hand.

Instantly she dropped to her knees to recover it, but it disappeared from view under the foaming edge of a wave.

"No!" Jessica cried, digging frantically in the wet sand.

"Jessica, come on!" Elizabeth called urgently.

"I lost it!" Jessica continued to dig as another clap of thunder shook the sky.

"It doesn't matter," Elizabeth shouted.

Jessica could barely hear her sister's voice above the roar of the storm, but she knew she couldn't leave until she found the necklace. It was dangerous to stay on the beach in this storm, but she didn't care.

"You go ahead, Elizabeth," she called.

Just then she caught a flash of red out of the corner of her eye. Her necklace! It was being carried out to sea again by a retreating wave. She made a desperate leap into the black water.

"Jessica!" she heard her sister scream.

Jessica couldn't see a thing. For a horrifying second she realized she might actually drown if she was sucked into the undertow by the ferocious storm. She clawed at the water, and suddenly her hand closed on something hard.

She'd found it. Holding the necklace, Jessica struggled back to the surface, fighting the waves that were trying to pull her out to sea. She staggered back onto dry land, sputtering and sucking in great gulps of air.

"Are you crazy?" Elizabeth yelled, running to her and grabbing her arm. "I can't believe you risked your life for that old piece of junk!"

"I had to get it," Jessica whispered, even though she couldn't have explained why, even to herself.

She opened her hand. A little more dirt had been washed away, and the red stone was easy to see now, illuminated by the eerie, flickering glow of lightning that split the sky overhead.

"Jessica, what *is* that thing?" Mrs. Wakefield asked later that evening as she came into the family room.

When Jessica didn't respond, Elizabeth shot her mother a meaningful look. "She's been this way ever since that director offered to let us be in the movie this afternoon," Elizabeth explained. "She must be dreaming of limousines and Hollywood parties."

"Jessica," Mrs. Wakefield said a little more loudly. "Are you still with us?"

Jessica was bent over the necklace she'd found,

carefully chipping off little flecks of the stubborn encrusted dirt that still coated it.

Steven, the twins' fourteen-year-old brother, grinned mischievously. "Jessica, I'm going to go call that director and tell her you've changed your mind about being in the movie, OK?"

When Jessica still didn't respond, Mr. Wakefield put down his paper and winked at his wife. "Those Hollywood types like Jessica are all alike," he remarked. "She's already forgotten us little people."

For a split second, Jessica looked over at her father. "I'm kind of busy, Dad," she said curtly.

"She found that necklace at the beach today," Elizabeth explained, "and she's been obsessed with trying to clean it ever since." She rolled her eyes. "In fact, she nearly drowned trying to rescue it when it fell in the ocean."

"Oh, well, maybe next time," Steven teased.

"Steven," Mrs. Wakefield said warningly. She down sat next to Jessica and reached for the necklace. "May I take a look, honey?"

"Hey!" Jessica said angrily as she tried to snatch it back.

"Jessica," Mrs. Wakefield exclaimed, raising her eyebrows. She held up the necklace and stared at it for a long time. "It could be very pretty," she said at last, "if we can just remove all those mineral deposits. I'll bet it was underwater for a very long time."

"I don't suppose that red stone's a ruby, is it?"

Mr. Wakefield asked with a wry smile.

"I doubt it, Ned." Mrs. Wakefield laughed. "A ruby that big would be worth a fortune. No, I think it's just a piece of costume jewelry."

"Costume jewelry?" Elizabeth asked.

"That's jewelry that may look very expensive, but is really just made with cheap stones or paste."

"A paste necklace?" Steven asked with a grimace. "Wouldn't that be kind of sticky?"

"Not that kind of paste. Paste is just a name they give to fake jewels." Mrs. Wakefield held the necklace up to the light. "Even if it's not worth much, there *is* something unique about it, isn't there?"

Elizabeth shook her head. "I don't see what the big deal is. Jessica practically got us both zapped by lightning just so she could hang on to the stupid thing."

"Still," Mrs. Wakefield said in a wistful voice, "there's something special about it . . ."

"It's mine," Jessica snapped, grabbing the necklace out of her mother's hand. "I found it, and that makes it mine."

Mrs. Wakefield blinked in surprise. "Jessica," she began. "I was only looking at—"

"I just want you all to know that this necklace is mine," Jessica interrupted, looking around at each of them in turn.

Elizabeth couldn't help staring at her sister. Jessica could be a little possessive sometimes, but this was ridiculous.

"Fine. *I* don't want it," Steven said with a shrug. "I don't think it goes with my eyes, do you?"

Elizabeth laughed and looked over at her sister. But Jessica didn't seem to have heard. Her head was already bent down over her necklace again.

By the time she went to bed that night, Jessica had cleaned off a second stone on the necklace. This one was smaller and perfectly clear, but it glittered even more brightly than the red stone. She would have thought it was a diamond if she didn't know better.

Tomorrow I'll finish cleaning it up, she promised herself as she climbed into bed. She slipped the necklace under her pillow, then reached over and snapped off the light.

It's been an amazing day, she thought sleepily. After all, it wasn't every day that she got hired as a movie extra. As great as that was, though, somehow it couldn't come close to her excitement about finding the necklace.

It bothered her a little that Elizabeth didn't share her enthusiasm for the necklace. At least her mother had seemed to understand how special it was.

Jessica reached under her pillow and closed her hand around the hard, uneven object. Maybe it was just as well that Elizabeth didn't understand. Jessica didn't want to share the necklace with anyone. *Even if it is just worthless costume jewelry,* she told herself, *it's mine. Mine.*

She lay there for a long time, clutching the necklace. Slowly her lids grew heavy, and she felt herself falling asleep. *Falling, falling, falling . . .*

She was falling backward. Her hands were clawing at the air. Her heart was pounding so hard, she was sure it was going to burst.

Above her loomed black storm clouds, racing across the sky. Lightning tore through the darkness, and in the brief flashes of light, she could see a face, then a hand. A voice shouted in triumph.

She wasn't falling anymore. She was running now, up a long staircase that twisted around and around. Something was wrong, terribly wrong.

Finally she stopped running. She felt as if she might even have stopped breathing. Her eyes locked on a glittering box of jewels. A hand—a strange hand—was digging deep into the box.

And then she was falling again. Falling backward, as black clouds closed in around her. Somehow she managed to twist her head around to catch a glimpse of the earth below. In a flash of lightning, she saw rocks rushing up to meet her, sharp and deadly.

Jessica screamed.

"Honey, are you all right?" Mr. Wakefield asked.

Jessica blinked, shielding her eyes from the light. She was lying in her safe comfortable bed, but she could still feel that terrifying sensation of falling. She could still see the rocks speeding toward her like huge, black daggers.

Elizabeth appeared in the doorway, pulling on a bathrobe. "Did you have a nightmare?" she asked sleepily.

Jessica sat up and forced herself to take a deep breath. The details of the nightmare were already fading a little. But she still felt a terrible sense of dread. "I guess so," she answered weakly.

Mrs. Wakefield sat down on the edge of the bed and felt Jessica's forehead. "Well, you don't have a fever," she said, "but you're bathed in sweat."

Jessica wiped the sleeve of her nightgown across her forehead. It was true. When she looked down at her hands, she was surprised to see that they were trembling.

"That was a serious scream," Elizabeth said. "What were you dreaming about?"

Jessica searched her memory. She remembered a hand filled with glittering jewels. There was something odd about the hand, but she couldn't quite recall what it was. And she clearly remembered falling.

"I dreamed I was falling," she said.

Mrs. Wakefield nodded. "I've had dreams like that. They're actually quite common. When you're having one it can be awfully scary."

Mr. Wakefield gave Jessica a reassuring hug. "See? Just a nightmare. I've had falling dreams too. Nothing to worry about, though." He bounced the springs of her bed. "You can't fall with a bed under you."

But I didn't have a bed under me, Jessica thought. *Only rocks.*

She remembered it all too clearly. Sharp, dagger-like rocks, and a swirling, boiling black sea. *It was the most vivid dream I've ever had,* she thought with a shiver.

Three

"You're not actually going to wear that thing to school today, are you?" Elizabeth asked as she waited impatiently in Jessica's doorway Tuesday morning.

Jessica gently placed the necklace in her backpack. "Of course not," she replied. "If I did, everyone would want it."

"You *are* kidding, I hope."

Jessica stifled a yawn. "I'm too tired to argue with you, Elizabeth. I didn't get a whole lot of sleep last night, you know."

"None of us did," Elizabeth said with a grin. "The next time you have a nightmare, try to make it a quiet one, OK?"

"I hope there never *is* a next one like that," Jessica said quietly.

Elizabeth glanced at her watch. "Come on. We're going to be late."

"One more thing." Jessica ran to her dresser and grabbed her sunglasses. "I may need these at school, now that I'm practically a movie star."

"What's the deal with the shades?" Lila Fowler demanded as soon as Jessica walked in the front door of Sweet Valley Middle School.

"Are you addressing *me*?" Jessica inquired, peering over the top of her sunglasses at her friend.

"Do you see anyone else walking around wearing sunglasses inside school? What are you supposed to be, some kind of movie star?" They stopped at Lila's locker and Lila began spinning the combination lock.

Jessica smiled tolerantly. "I expected this. It can be difficult when people with true talent succeed, and their friends are left behind." There was nothing Jessica loved more than bragging to Lila. That was because Lila did so much bragging herself. Her father was one of the wealthiest people in Sweet Valley, and in Jessica's opinion, he spoiled Lila rotten.

But Lila wasn't even paying attention. She was too busy yanking on the door of her locker. When it wouldn't open, she kicked it so hard the noise echoed down the hallway.

"Hey, what's with the sunglasses?" Ellen Riteman asked as she joined them. She turned to Lila. "And why are you beating on your locker?"

Lila leaned against the locker door, looking exasperated. "I forgot my stupid combination again."

"It's 13-22-9," Ellen said matter-of-factly.

"Thanks," Lila said. She began to twirl the lock, then stopped. "Wait a minute. How come you know my locker combination?"

"Everyone knows your locker combination, Lila. We all use your mousse when we run out."

"Ex*cuse* me? You use *my* mousse, from *my* locker?" Lila cried in an outraged voice.

"Sure. You're rich. You can afford to share," Ellen said reasonably.

"If you little people could please forget the mousse for a minute—" Jessica began, seeing her big moment slipping away.

"I'd better not ever catch you going into my locker again, Ellen!" Lila yelled.

"Jessica does it too," Ellen pointed out defensively.

"Is that true, Jessica?" Lila demanded, hands on her hips. "And take off those silly sunglasses. I want to be able to see your eyes, so I can tell if you're lying."

"Even if you could see my eyes," Jessica replied, "you wouldn't be able to tell if I was lying. I'm way too good an actress for that. And speaking of acting—"

"What are you yelling about?" Janet Howell demanded as she walked over. Janet was president of the Unicorns, a position she took very seriously. "I could hear you screeching all the way down the hall, Lila. People are staring."

"These two have been opening my locker—my *private* locker—and using my mousse," Lila cried.

"So what? I do it too." Janet frowned at Jessica. "Jessica, take off those ridiculous sunglasses," she said. "What do you think you are, some kind of movie star or something?"

"Well, actually—"

"OK, OK. Stop arguing about Lila's dumb mousse," Janet said impatiently. "I've got something really important to tell you. Ready for this? Belinda heard from Mandy who heard from Caroline that they're making a movie out at the Keller mansion. You know, the big old place at the end of the beach?"

"I know," Jessica exclaimed.

"Good for you, Jessica. We all know where it is," Janet said dismissively. "Anyway, Caroline heard they're going to be looking for extras." She lowered her voice dramatically. "Mostly they're looking for a lot of girls—*middle-school-aged girls*—which could mean us!"

"I've been trying to tell you—" Jessica began.

"How do we find out about getting to be extras?" Lila asked excitedly.

"Go to the Keller mansion tomorrow afternoon—"

"—and bring a permission letter from—" Jessica

managed to interject before she was cut off by the loud ringing of the first-period bell.

"Uh oh. Gotta go," Lila said.

"Wait," Jessica cried. "Don't you want to hear why I'm wearing sunglasses?"

"Can't," Lila replied. "If I'm late again, I'll get a detention for sure."

"Me too," Janet said.

"Me three," Ellen agreed.

Jessica watched in disbelief as her friends disappeared into the stream of kids rushing to class. *Great*, she thought, annoyed. *I didn't even get to gloat.*

Just before she reached her first-period class, Jessica remembered to pull off her sunglasses. As she folded them up and stuck them in her backpack, her hand brushed against the necklace. She stopped in midstride. She really couldn't afford to be late to class either. But she just had to take a quick look.

Jessica ducked into the girls' bathroom. Fortunately, it was empty. She set her bag down on the counter and opened it. Inside she could see a glint of red.

She pulled out the necklace and stared at it for a long time. With her fingernail, she began to scrape again at the hard sediment covering the chain. Eventually she managed to pry a tiny piece loose. She could see that there was another stone beneath it, but she couldn't be sure of the color.

This was taking much too long. She fumbled in her bag for a nail file. She began to scrape at the necklace with it, trying not to damage anything. Slowly the third jewel became visible. It was clear and sparkling.

"What are you doing in here?"

Jessica looked up with a start. Ms. Mendez, the new assistant principal, was standing in the doorway, looking at Jessica with obvious suspicion.

"Do you have a hall pass?" Ms. Mendez demanded.

Jessica clutched the necklace in her fist. "Um, no, not exactly. I kind of . . . got distracted. Sorry about that. I guess I'll be going to class now." She made a dive toward the door.

"Distracted?" Ms. Mendez echoed. "First period is half over. That's a long distraction."

Jessica stopped in her tracks. "Half over? That can't be. I—"

Ms. Mendez shook her head. "I don't know why I should let you go for this, but the truth is, I'm just not in the mood to write up a detention slip right now. I'll leave it to your first-period teacher to decide what to do with you." She shook her finger at Jessica. "But don't ever let me catch you getting 'distracted' like this again."

"I promise," Jessica vowed. She dashed out the door, holding on tightly to the necklace. When she'd turned the corner, she paused to gaze with satisfaction at the shiny new stone. So what if the necklace had almost gotten her into trouble? It was worth it.

"The whole school must be here," Jessica marveled. It was Wednesday afternoon, and nearly a hundred kids had lined up in front of the Keller mansion, hoping to be chosen as extras.

Today, in the bright sunshine, the mansion didn't seem frightening at all. In fact, with its new coat of white paint, it almost looked inviting. "Come on. Let's go to the front of the line," Jessica whispered, grabbing Elizabeth's arm.

"Why should you go to the front?" Lila protested.

"Since Elizabeth and I are already hired, I don't see why we should have to stand in line with all you amateurs," Jessica said haughtily.

"You're *hired*? What are you talking about?" Lila demanded.

"Nobody's been hired yet," Janet said.

Jessica waited until every Unicorn's attention was focused on her. "Lizzie and I were here on Monday afternoon. The director immediately spotted my true talent, and signed us up." Jessica smiled modestly. It was wonderful finally to get a chance to brag.

"No way," Lila said.

"You are so lucky," Ellen exclaimed.

"That's fantastic," Maria Slater said. Maria was

standing near the Unicorns with Elizabeth.

"Since when do *you* want to be an actress, Elizabeth?" Lila demanded.

"I don't," Elizabeth answered truthfully.

"I sort of talked the director into letting Elizabeth come along too," Jessica said quickly. "Becka obviously spotted my talent right away—that's what makes her such a great director, I guess. Anyway, Elizabeth wanted to do a little article for the paper, and Becka decided as a favor to me that it would be all right."

"I'm *sure* that's *exactly* what happened," Maria said, exchanging a grin with Elizabeth. Maria had acted in TV shows and movies when she was younger. "Of course, the fact that you two are twins may also have had something to do with it."

"What's that got to do with anything?" Ellen asked.

"Becka explained that kids our age are allowed to work only a certain number of hours a day," Elizabeth replied. "If they have identical twins, they can double the time they can use them."

"That's right," Maria agreed. "Directors love twins. When I was working, we'd sometimes have to stop shooting right in the middle of things because I had worked all I was allowed to for that day."

"So the director obviously spotted your talent, huh?" Lila said to Jessica. "She could spot the fact that you two are identical, that's what she could spot."

Janet shook her head. "I can't believe this."

"What? That I'm going to be in the movie?" Jessica said triumphantly. "It's really not so hard to believe, considering—"

"No," Janet snapped. "I can't believe that you didn't tell us. You've known about this since *Monday*? What kind of Unicorn are you, anyway?"

"Too young," Becka Silver muttered as she passed the first girl in line. Murray and the others nodded in agreement. "Too tall," Becka remarked as she walked by the next girl.

"*That's* the director?" Lila whispered. "She looks like the actress who used to be on that really dumb TV comedy."

"That is her," Maria Slater confirmed. "Now she directs."

Jessica heard "too sweet," "too mature," and "too exotic" before Becka stopped in front of Lila and looked her over carefully.

"I'm a big fan of yours," Lila blurted. "I used to love that TV show you were on. Especially the way you were always the dweeb and got into really stupid messes, and the girl who played your friend would always say something really hysterical. It used to crack me up."

Becka raised an eyebrow.

Maria winced. "Becka hated that other actress," she whispered to Jessica.

"Excuse me," Becka said coolly, "but *I* was the funny one on that show."

Lila swallowed. "That's what I meant."

"Uh-huh," Becka muttered doubtfully. "Anyway, we can't use you. Sorry."

"Wait!" Lila said frantically. "Why not?"

"Because you opened your big mouth, Lila," Jessica said triumphantly.

Becka laughed. "No, it's because you have what we call a modern face. This movie is set in the 1940's. You look too contemporary to fit in." She moved past Lila, then paused in front of Jessica and Elizabeth. "Ah, my twins," Becka said. She turned to Murray. "We're going to use these two as Luella, the neighbor's daughter. We have several scenes with that character." She gazed at them each in turn. "Either of you have any experience? The part has about two lines of dialogue."

"Well, nothing *professional*, exactly," Jessica admitted, "but I do subscribe to all the movie magazines, and I'm planning on becoming a star someday."

Becka sighed. "I guess that'll have to do. Someone will arrange for you to get a copy of the script eventually."

Jessica couldn't help giving the Unicorns a superior smile.

Becka was already heading down the line, but Jessica had just remembered something she'd been meaning to ask.

"Um, Becka?" she called timidly. She wasn't sure extras were allowed to call directors by their first names, and she didn't want to start her career off on the wrong foot.

"Yeah?"

"Can I ask you something?"

"Sure. Fire away."

"What's this movie about?"

"It's about two girls your age," Becka replied. "A pretty wild story, actually."

"Like an adventure movie?" Jessica asked hopefully.

"Not exactly. More like a murder mystery."

"What happens to the girls?" Jessica pressed.

"One turns out to be a killer."

"What about the other one?" Jessica asked.

"She turns out to be dead."

Jessica tried to scream, but when she opened her mouth, no sound came out. She tried to turn and run, but her feet seemed to be glued to the floor.

She looked down and saw that she was wearing an old pair of black leather shoes. These aren't my shoes, Jessica thought anxiously. I wouldn't be caught dead wearing shoes like these.

She heard a sound nearby. She looked up and saw a hand digging into a box of glittering jewels—gold and silver, diamonds and emeralds, sapphires and rubies. Something about the hand was odd, and a little frightening.

But she didn't have time to think about it, because suddenly she was running. She wasn't really afraid.

Was she angry? Yes, that was it. She'd been happy and someone had upset her. She was running away from the person who had made her angry.

As she ran, something heavy was scraping on her collar. Something heavy that felt cold against the bare skin of her throat.

Suddenly she was hanging from a precipice, her body rigid with fear, her fingers aching with the effort of trying to hold on. Then, all at once, she was falling.

Overhead the sky was black, torn by jagged bolts of lightning. She twisted her neck, straining to see, and in a brilliant flash of lightning she saw the sharp rocks rushing up toward her.

She felt a terrible blow. Her eyes closed as the icy black water clutched at her.

"No!" Jessica cried, and this time she found her voice. She sat bolt upright in her bed. Her heart was pounding as she reached over and snapped on her bedside lamp.

Everything in her room was right where it should be—the posters on her walls, the clothing strewn around on the floor, the little ceramic unicorn that she kept on her dresser. The glowing green numbers on her clock said 3:36.

"Another nightmare," she whispered to herself. At least this time she hadn't awakened the whole house.

Jessica reached under her pillow and pulled out the necklace, clutching it in her sweaty hand as she tried to catch her breath. She'd spent all evening cleaning it, chipping away at the dirt and minerals.

She held it under the light and examined it. The large red stone was completely clean, and so were six smaller stones. Soon she would have to clean off the clasp so that she could try the necklace on. But for now, all she could do was imagine how it would look.

She gazed in her dresser mirror, holding up the necklace. It was cold—very cold—against the bare skin of her throat

Four

Elizabeth had to admit that Mrs. Arnette, even on her good days, could be a little boring. And this definitely wasn't one of her good days.

Mrs. Arnette was the sixth-grade social studies teacher, and social studies was one of Elizabeth's favorite subjects. But today the lesson was about how a bill becomes a law, and even Elizabeth was having a hard time staying awake. Maybe it was because tomorrow was Friday, the last day before spring break began. Or maybe it was the way Mrs. Arnette's voice seemed to drone on like a fly buzzing back and forth across the room.

"So then the bill is reported on by a committee," Mrs. Arnette was saying. "A committee of the Senate, if the bill is in the Senate, or a committee of the House of Representatives, if the bill is in the

House of Representatives. Of course, if the Senate and the House have both passed slightly different versions of the same bill, then they have to compromise on the differences, in which case the bill is sent to a joint committee composed of members from both the . . ."

Elizabeth's eyelids were growing heavy. She sat up straighter and glanced over at her twin. It was obvious that Jessica was fighting to stay awake too, and losing the battle.

Poor Jess, Elizabeth thought. Jessica hadn't been sleeping well at all the past couple days. This morning at breakfast she had said that she'd had another awful nightmare.

Elizabeth watched her twin's eyes flutter closed and her head droop forward. A moment later, Jessica jerked back up, safely awake again, at least for a little while.

Elizabeth wondered if Jessica's nightmares were the reason she'd been acting so strangely this week. Jessica hardly seemed excited at all that she'd been chosen to be in a movie, or that spring vacation was just around the corner. She spent all her time walking around like a sleepy zombie, or cleaning off that stupid necklace she'd found at the beach.

Amy Sutton, Elizabeth's best friend, reached across the aisle and nudged Elizabeth. Then she inclined her head in Jessica's direction.

"I saw," Elizabeth whispered.

"There she goes again," Amy whispered with a grin. "She'll be out cold in five minutes."

"There's nothing I can do. She's too far away," Elizabeth whispered back, shrugging helplessly.

When Mrs. Arnette turned to face the board, Elizabeth waved to catch Lila's eye. Lila was sitting close enough to Jessica to nudge her awake. When Lila finally looked over, Elizabeth pointed frantically at Jessica. Lila turned around just in time to see Jessica falling forward yet again, her forehead only inches from her desktop. Lila turned back toward Elizabeth and calmly spread her hands, palms up.

"Why won't she wake her up?" Amy asked in a whisper.

"Lila didn't get hired for the movie. I don't think she's taking it well," Elizabeth replied.

Just then, Jessica's head drifted down onto the desktop. This time she didn't come back up.

"Maybe the Hairnet won't notice," Amy suggested.

Elizabeth sighed. She was afraid that even Mrs. Arnette would be sure to notice that one of her students was completely passed out on her desk.

To make matters worse, Jessica suddenly groaned softly. Fortunately, Mrs. Arnette was still at the blackboard, drawing a chalk diagram of a bill's progress through Congress.

Jessica made a little whimpering noise.

This time Mrs. Arnette paused, her chalk

poised in midair. Elizabeth held her breath. To her relief, Mrs. Arnette went back to drawing lines on the board. Jessica was lucky, that was for sure.

"AH, AH, AHHHHHHHHH!"

Elizabeth's heart plunged. It was a scream of pure terror, and it was coming from Jessica.

Jessica's head shot up. "AHHHHHHHH! NO! NO!" she cried, as Mrs. Arnette spun around and the whole class turned to stare.

Slowly Jessica opened her eyes. Even from across the room, Elizabeth could see that Jessica's face was pale with fear. Jessica's hands shook as she gripped the edge of her desk.

Elizabeth jumped to her feet and ran to her sister's side. "Are you all right?" she asked, putting a comforting arm around Jessica's shoulders.

Jessica gulped, then gave a tentative smile. "Just a nightmare," she said softly. "No big deal."

There was nervous laughter from some of the other students. Elizabeth couldn't really blame them. Jessica's cry had been horrifying.

"I think you'd better go see the school nurse," Mrs. Arnette said, sounding concerned. "You look a little pale."

"I'm fine," Jessica protested weakly.

"Go. She's just down the hall, so you won't need a pass," Mrs. Arnette said, sounding a little unnerved herself.

"Go on, Jess," Elizabeth said, patting her sister

on the back. "Maybe you'll luck out and get sent home early."

"Brilliant idea, Jessica," Winston Egbert joked. "I think I'll try that nightmare trick during English class."

Winston's joke seemed to break some of the tension in the room. Slowly Jessica climbed to her feet. She was almost to the door when she paused and turned back. "My backpack," she said urgently.

"I'll take care of it for you," Elizabeth reassured her.

"No." Jessica frowned. "I have to—"

"Go, Jessica," Mrs. Arnette ordered. "Right now."

Jessica reached out her hand toward the bag, but then, with a reluctant sigh, she turned away and disappeared down the hall.

As soon as class let out, Elizabeth grabbed her backpack, along with Jessica's, and ran for the nurse's office. But Jessica was gone.

"I decided to send her home," explained Ms. Walsh, the school nurse. "She admitted she'd had trouble sleeping last night, which explains why she fell asleep in class. And with only one more day until spring break, I didn't see much harm in sending her home to rest."

"So it was just a nightmare?" Elizabeth asked.

"Of course. What else would it be?" Ms. Walsh smiled reassuringly. "Nightmares aren't something you need to worry about. Everybody has them now and then. I've had some real doozies myself."

Elizabeth thanked the nurse and headed toward the library. She wanted to do some research on the Keller mansion before her next class. If she was going to do a good interview with Becka, Elizabeth knew it would help to have some background information on the mansion's history.

When she got to the library, Elizabeth flopped both backpacks down beside her and began checking the index for anything under the name "Keller." It took twenty minutes before she found something interesting—she had to go all the way back to a newspaper article from 1939.

Elizabeth grabbed her bags and selected a spool of microfilm that contained copies of the *The Sweet Valley Tribune* for March 1939. Elizabeth had plenty of experience in the library, so she was able to load the microfilm spool without any problem. After turning on the view light, she carefully advanced the spool to the right month and day and read the headline at the top of the page: KELLER HEIRESS DIES TRAGICALLY.

Elizabeth reached into her backpack for a pencil so she could take notes. On the bottom of the bag, she felt something odd. She glanced down and realized she was reaching into Jessica's bag instead of her own.

Elizabeth started to pull her hand out, then hesitated. There was something interesting about the object her fingers had brushed against. Elizabeth couldn't resist looking to see what it was.

It was the necklace Jessica had found in the surf. *How strange*, Elizabeth thought. Had Jessica been taking it to school like this all week?

She stared at necklace. Most of it was still encrusted with minerals, dirt, and tiny shells, but Jessica had cleaned up several of the stones. Elizabeth gazed at the shimmering stones in fascination. She couldn't believe Jessica hadn't shown it to her after cleaning it off.

One thing was certain—Jessica would never forgive her if Elizabeth lost the necklace. It would be a whole lot safer in her pocket, Elizabeth decided. She could easily forget Jessica's backpack, after all. She slipped the necklace into her pocket and looked back at the screen.

KELLER HEIRESS IN FATAL ACCIDENT

Lillian Keller, heir to the Keller fortune, died tragically yesterday only minutes after celebrating her twelfth birthday. She is believed to have fallen from a balcony at the Keller mansion that overlooked the shoreline. Though Miss Keller's body was washed some distance out to sea, it has been recovered.

There is no suggestion of foul play, but witnesses at the party say that Miss Keller had fought over a gift with Hilda Tomlinson, also twelve years of age, immediately before her death. Miss Tomlinson, a cousin of the deceased, is an orphan who was taken in by the Keller family one year ago. The family had no comment on the tragedy. Mrs. Keller, the victim's mother, is reported to be under a doctor's care.

"Poor Lillian," Elizabeth whispered. She looked away from the screen. It was a terribly sad story. And after what Becka had said to Jessica the day before, Elizabeth had a strong feeling the movie was going to have something to do with Lillian's death.

"Hey, you two, this is supposed to be a party," Jessica announced as soon as Elizabeth stepped through the door that afternoon.

Elizabeth checked over her shoulder. Just as she'd thought, no one else was there. "Jessica? What are you talking about?" she asked gently. Maybe Jessica hadn't quite recovered from her nightmare yet.

"Wait!" Jessica called out, throwing her hands in the air. "We *still* haven't cut the cake!"

"Jessica, maybe you should sit down for a while," Elizabeth suggested.

"How about if I put the emphasis more on the word *cake*, like this—Wait! We still haven't cut the *cake*!"

"Jessica," Elizabeth said, "what exactly did the nurse tell you today?"

"Oh, she said I was probably just tired." Jessica shrugged. "But who cares about that? I have acting to do! Lines to memorize!"

"Are you telling me these are *lines*? From the movie?"

"Of course." Jessica rolled her eyes. "Do you think I'm just wandering around the house talking about parties and cakes for no reason?"

"You mean Becka sent the script over?"

"By messenger," Jessica said proudly.

"Where is it?"

"Over there, on the coffee table."

Elizabeth turned toward the coffee table eagerly. The script would answer all her questions about the movie, and whether it really was about the death of Lillian Keller.

Unfortunately, all she found on the table was one sheet of paper. "Is this it?" she demanded. "Where's the rest?"

Jessica shrugged. "Well, it's not like I have a lot of lines. I mean, this *is* my first acting job. I can't expect to be the star right away. Becka only sent the page that had the lines I'm supposed to learn. In my next picture I'll have a bigger role."

Elizabeth slumped on the couch, feeling a little disappointed. "Actually, I should learn those lines too," she said unenthusiastically. "We don't know which one of us is going to end up doing which scene."

Jessica frowned. "Wait!" she said suddenly. "We still haven't *cut* the cake!"

Elizabeth couldn't help smiling. "You seem to be in a better mood," she observed.

"What do you mean?"

"I don't know. It's just that this is the first time you've seemed excited about the movie."

"Of course I'm excited!" Jessica exclaimed. "This is the greatest thing that's ever happened to me in my whole life."

"I guess you've just been tired," Elizabeth said. "What with all the nightmares."

A shadow passed over Jessica's face. "I *was* feeling kind of weird." She shrugged, instantly brightening. "But now I'm fine."

"I can see that," Elizabeth said. "I guess playing hooky really perked you up." She stood and picked up her backpack and the page of script. After a moment's hesitation, she picked up Jessica's bag too.

"Hey, thanks for bringing my stuff home," Jessica said. "I hope you forgot to bring any homework."

"No problem." Elizabeth paused, looking down at her sister's bag with a strange twinge of guilt. "I—I happened to see that thing in your bag."

"What thing?"

"That necklace."

Jessica's eyes darkened at the mention of the necklace.

"I guess you want it back?"

Jessica hesitated. "I guess so," she said tentatively.

Elizabeth reached into her pocket and held the glittering necklace. Jessica began to reach for it, but at the last moment she pulled her hand away as Elizabeth tightened her grip around the chain.

"You know," Jessica said in a faraway, thoughtful voice. "I don't really want it anymore."

"Can I have it?" Elizabeth demanded. She was surprised at the anxiousness in her own voice.

"I guess so," Jessica said, giving her an odd look.

Elizabeth quickly slipped the necklace into her own pocket. Jessica broke into a relieved smile.

In her pocket, the necklace was cold against Elizabeth's fingertips. She headed upstairs to her room. As she climbed the stairs, she glanced over the page of script she was holding.

ACT TWO, it read. *Keller mansion ballroom. LIL-LIAN, HILDA, and several friends have gathered for Lillian's birthday party.*

Elizabeth paused. So the movie *was* about the death of Lillian Keller, after all.

"Wait! *We* still haven't cut the cake!" Jessica called, but Elizabeth didn't answer.

Five

"It's not yours," Elizabeth cried angrily. "It's mine. My mother gave it to me."

She was in a huge, high-ceilinged, candlelit room, screaming at a girl with brown pigtails. Elizabeth and the other girl were both wearing old-fashioned dresses.

Elizabeth had never been so furious. Blind with rage, she ran up a long flight of stairs. Behind her, someone called out, "Don't run off. There's ice cream!"

There was a loud clap of thunder as Elizabeth reached the top of the stairs and ran down a hallway. She turned a corner and heard a rustling sound. For a second she was sure it must be her mother. But it wasn't.

The sound came from necklaces and bracelets and earrings—all sorts of fantastic jewels being shoved around in a box. She saw the jewels, and saw the hand that was in the box.

Strange, *Elizabeth thought*. There are only four.
Suddenly she backed away. Her anger had turned to intense fear. Behind her, she felt something solid, and then there was nothing but air, and she was falling, her screams lost in the howling wind . . .

"Noooooo!" Elizabeth woke up panting, clutching the damp sheet to her pounding heart. She snapped on the light. The warm yellow glow of the lamp was instantly reassuring.

She looked around, gratefully taking in the familiar surroundings. Her eyes fell on her nightstand, where the one page of Becka's movie script lay. Under it was the copy of the newspaper article she had found in the library.

Elizabeth took a deep breath. "You shouldn't be reading articles about murder right before you go to sleep, Elizabeth Wakefield," she muttered.

Obviously, her dream had something to do with the newspaper story. Lillian Keller had fallen to her death. That explained the terrifying fall at the end of her nightmare. Of course, in her dream, the details were a little different, but that was normal. That was just how dreams were.

She picked up the page of script. There were only a few lines on it, with no explanation of what had happened earlier in the scene.

LILLIAN: My mother would never give me something that didn't rightly belong to her.

HILDA: But she has. I know. I've seen it many times before, around her neck when she went out to parties.

LUELLA: Hey, you two. This is supposed to be a party.

LILLIAN: *(ignoring Luella and keeping her gaze fixed on Hilda)* You're just lying because you're jealous. It's mine. My mother gave it to me.

HILDA: *(determined)* But it belonged to my mother. My mother!

LILLIAN: *(very angry)* You're being awful. I hate you! *(runs away suddenly)*

LUELLA: Wait! We still haven't cut the cake!

HILDA: *(in a whisper as she watches Lillian run off)* I'll never let her have it. Never, never, never!

Elizabeth set down the page. It was just as she'd suspected. Her dream had been just a replay of the scene. It was comforting to know that.

Still, it was funny how the mind worked. In the script, Luella mentioned cake. In Elizabeth's dream, she'd mentioned ice cream.

Elizabeth shrugged and snapped off her light. The nightmare bug seemed to be catching in the Wakefield house. She stuck her hand under her pillow and felt the cool stones of the necklace. It took her a long time to fall back to sleep.

*   *   *

Jessica awoke feeling absolutely terrific. *And why shouldn't I?* she thought with a grin as she jumped out of bed. Spring break was only a few hours away, and she was about to become a movie star. What more could a girl ask for—except maybe an extra-big bowl of Corny-O's, her favorite cereal? For some reason, she felt as though she hadn't eaten in days.

She dressed quickly and headed downstairs for breakfast. For what may have been the first time in history, she actually got to the table before Elizabeth. Mrs. Wakefield was sipping a cup of coffee while Mr. Wakefield muttered about the sports scores in the morning newspaper. Steven was leaning across the table, trying to read the back of the paper.

"Where's Elizabeth?" Jessica asked.

"She hasn't come down yet," Mrs. Wakefield said. "I wonder if she overslept. She's usually here at least ten minutes before you."

Jessica was on her second helping of Corny-O's when Elizabeth trudged into the kitchen.

"What happened?" Mrs. Wakefield asked Elizabeth. "Didn't your alarm go off?"

Elizabeth shrugged and slipped into the chair beside Jessica. "It went off, but then I fell back to sleep. I guess I was tired."

"How can you be tired?" Jessica asked excitedly. "Only a few more hours till freedom, Elizabeth! And don't forget the movie."

At the mention of the movie, Elizabeth furrowed her brow, as though she were trying to remember something. "I guess you're right," she said at last, managing a small smile.

"I've got something else that should perk you up," Mrs. Wakefield said. "I wanted to wait until you were both here to tell you. Your Aunt Nancy called from San Diego early this morning. I mentioned that you two were going to be extras in a movie production, and she said that Robin would love to come down for a visit during the break."

"Oh, great!" Jessica said melodramatically. "Now that I'm a star, *everyone* wants to be around me. This is always the way it happens. I suppose she wants me to use my influence to get her a job as an extra too."

"She's coming in by bus tomorrow," Mrs. Wakefield said, laughing. "I'm sure you won't mind sharing a little of your glory."

Jessica smiled. "Actually, it'll be really fun having Robin here. We always have a good time when she visits. Right, Lizzie?"

Elizabeth smiled vaguely. "Sure. It'll be nice."

That afternoon, Elizabeth sat impatiently through science class, watching the minutes tick away on the big clock behind Ms. Blake's desk. It wasn't that she was anxious for vacation to begin. Unlike everyone else in school, she hadn't really given it much thought. Elizabeth wanted class to end so she could ask Ms. Blake a very important question.

When the bell finally rang, the class broke into cheers. Elizabeth waited until everyone else had rushed out of the room before approaching Ms. Blake, who was erasing the blackboard.

"Um, Ms. Blake?" she said tentatively. "Could I ask you a question? A science question?"

"I'm impressed," Ms. Blake said with a grin. "Spring vacation just officially started, and you're still thinking about science." She sighed. "Why can't all my students be so dedicated?"

"This is kind of a strange question, I guess, but I found an old . . . an old thing."

"What kind of old thing?"

"It's a, um—" Elizabeth searched her mind desperately. She should have thought this through a little better. She wasn't exactly a pro at lying—that was Jessica's specialty. In fact, Elizabeth had never lied to a teacher before. But there was no way she could tell Ms. Blake about the necklace. She might ask to see it, and once Ms. Blake got hold of it, she might want to keep the necklace for herself. Elizabeth couldn't take that risk. The necklace was *hers*.

Ms. Blake set down her eraser. "Is it animal, vegetable, or mineral?"

"Mineral," Elizabeth replied. "It's an, uh, old bottle—a really old bottle that washed up out of the ocean. It looks like it's been in the water for a long time. It's covered in hard deposits that are kind of like a crust. And there are little tiny shells all over it."

Ms. Blake nodded. "The little shells are probably barnacles. They attach themselves to things in the water. The other deposits may be any number of minerals or salts that gradually built up over the years. That's quite normal."

Elizabeth sighed in relief. So far, Ms. Blake believed her story. "Well, I was wondering if there was something I could use to clean the bottle off."

"Good idea," Ms. Blake said. "Sometimes old bottles can be valuable as collector's items." She thought for a moment. "Well, we have some solvents down in the science lab that would probably help dissolve the deposits."

"Really?"

Ms. Blake nodded again and rattled off the names of two chemicals. "You know, if you bring the bottle in when school starts again after vacation, I'll be glad to show you how to do it."

"I wouldn't want to take up your time," Elizabeth said quickly.

"No problem for one of my favorite students," Ms. Blake said affectionately. "Besides, you have to be careful with some of those chemicals."

Elizabeth checked up and down the hallway to make sure no one was watching. She didn't have to worry—everyone had already taken off right after the bell, leaving the halls completely deserted. Fortunately, Jessica had made plans to go to the mall with the Unicorns, so she wouldn't be waiting to walk home with Elizabeth.

Elizabeth slipped into the science lab and eased the door shut behind her. The room was dark, lit only by the sunlight filtering through a small window. Microscopes lined one wall, and other scientific equipment filled another wall of shelves. In one corner sat a row of gangly plants grown from avocado pits.

Elizabeth knew her way around the lab room well. She'd often helped Ms. Blake to prepare experiments for class. The cabinet with all the chemicals was kept locked, but Elizabeth knew exactly where the key was kept. She had to climb onto a chair to reach the little key's hiding place, on a ledge over the doorway.

She opened the cabinet and began searching the labels on the brown bottles inside for the names of the chemicals Ms. Blake had mentioned.

"There you are," she whispered, after a few minutes of frantic searching. The bottle was on the top shelf of the cabinet, and she had to climb up onto a counter to reach it. Holding the bottle steady, she carefully clambered down.

She took the bottle over to a sink and gazed at the warning label. *Do not ingest,* she read. *Avoid contact with skin or eyes.* A wave of guilt washed over her. It wasn't like her to be doing this.

Chemicals could be dangerous, and if anyone found out about this, she could be expelled from school.

She reached into her pocket and pulled out the necklace. *I have to do this*, she told herself.

She unscrewed the bottle top carefully. *Phew*, she thought. *They should have added a warning about the smell.*

She put the necklace into a small glass dish in the sink and slowly poured a few tablespoons of the solvent onto it. Immediately it began to smoke, and there was a soft hissing sound.

"Oh, no!" Elizabeth cried. She quickly turned on the faucet, drenching the necklace with water.

Her hands were shaking as she lifted the necklace out of the dish. *What if I've hurt it?* she wondered frantically. But when she examined the necklace, she was relieved to see that it didn't appear to be damaged. In fact, three more small, clear stones had been uncovered, and the remaining deposits at the edges of the large red stone had been cleaned away. *Thank goodness it's okay*, she thought, letting out a sigh.

Just then, as she held the necklace, the red stone dropped out of its silver setting onto the counter.

Elizabeth stared in horror. The solvent must have loosened the glue behind the stone. On closer examination, she noticed that one of the silver prongs that should have held the red stone in place was broken off. Maybe she or Jessica had broken it while they were cleaning the necklace earlier.

Just then, something new caught her eye. Tiny ornate letters were engraved into the silver in the spot where the red stone had been.

"J.K.T." Elizabeth read aloud. Those must have been the initials of the necklace's owner, she figured. "J.K.T.," Elizabeth repeated. "I wonder who you are—or *were*?"

She put the necklace back into her pocket, along with the red stone. As soon as she got home, she'd glue the stone back into place.

Elizabeth put the top back on the bottle of solvent, and carefully climbed back up onto the countertop. She'd had enough of experimenting with science for one day.

She returned the solvent to its shelf. As she climbed back down off the counter, she lost her balance and slipped. Before she could grab anything, she was falling backward.

As she fell toward the floor, she closed her eyes and saw a flash of a stormy sky torn by jagged lightning. A face, darkened by shadows, seemed to watch her as she fell.

"Ow!" she yelled as she hit the floor. Her eyes blinked open and she paused for a moment to catch her breath before climbing unsteadily to her feet. She was going to have a bruise that would make it uncomfortable to sit down for a while, Elizabeth thought ruefully, but otherwise she was OK.

But what was it she'd seen as she was falling? Was it a memory? A dream? The scene had seemed so real—and so terrifying.

Elizabeth shook her head. "The smell of that solvent is probably making me light-headed," she said aloud to make herself feel better. But the eerie memory of that shadowy face stayed with her all the way home.

Six

"Stand still, honey, I'm trying to measure your waist." Jessica stopped fidgeting and stood still as Nadia, the wardrobe woman, wrapped a tape measure around her waist. It was Saturday morning, and the twins were being fitted for their costumes in one of the trailers that ringed the Keller mansion.

"I've been trying to tell you," Jessica repeated for what seemed like the hundredth time, "I'm exactly the same size as Elizabeth. We're twins."

"Kid, I don't know any Elizabeth, all right?"

"But you just measured her two minutes ago. We're twins. We're exactly the same size."

For the first time, Nadia looked up from her tape measure. Jessica pointed out the open trailer door to Elizabeth, who was waiting outside.

"Hey," Nadia exclaimed, "you two *are* twins. How

come nobody told me? I'm wasting my time." She tossed aside her tape measure and reached for her clipboard. "Nobody tells me anything around here," she muttered. Quickly she copied the figures she'd written down for Elizabeth under Jessica's name too.

"Am I done?" Jessica asked.

"Yep. Send in the next kid, would ya?"

Jessica sighed as she walked down the trailer steps into the bright sunlight. This wasn't exactly what she'd had in mind for her first day of stardom. Whatever happened to *lights, camera, action*? When did she get to show off her moving interpretation of what had to be the most important line of dialogue in the entire movie?

"Wait!" Jessica murmured. "We *still* haven't cut the cake!"

"Did you say something?" Elizabeth asked.

Before Jessica could answer, a tall man named Rolf waved at the twins. "This way," he called, motioning them toward the entrance to the mansion.

"*Finally*," Jessica exclaimed as she grabbed Elizabeth's arm. "It's showtime!"

Rolf led the girls inside the mansion to a huge ballroom where all the action seemed to be focused.

"It's a real, live movie set," Jessica said excitedly. She gazed around the ballroom in amazement. Dozens of huge lights hung from the ceiling, and miles of cable crisscrossed all over the floor like huge snakes. Two big cameras on dollies sat in one corner of the room. Men and women in overalls bustled about purposefully. Some were hanging a crystal chandelier in the center of the room, and others were carefully placing fake bricks over the real bricks around the fireplace. A chill ran up Jessica's spine, and she realized there was something eerily familiar about the room.

"Wait here," Rolf commanded. "And don't get into any mischief."

"What happens next?" Jessica asked, shaking off her momentary feeling of dread.

"Darling, I wish I knew," Rolf said, rolling his eyes before he dashed off.

"It's hard to believe that people actually lived in this house," Elizabeth said softly.

Jessica nodded. "It makes Lila's house look like a dump."

"Coming through!" yelled a workman carrying a long ladder as he nearly beheaded a young woman speaking into a walkie-talkie.

Jessica shook her head. "This place doesn't seem very well organized, does it?"

Behind her, Jessica heard laughter. She turned and saw an old man leaning against the wall. Like many of the other workmen, he was dressed in overalls. He had one hand in his pocket, and in the other hand he held the glowing butt of a cigarette.

The old man smiled slightly. "I didn't mean to eavesdrop," he said. "But what you said struck me as funny. Not to mention true. It does seem very disorganized, doesn't it?"

"Well, it's not like I'm an expert on movie-making or anything," Jessica said quickly. There was no point in insulting the employees on her very first day.

"No, I didn't think you were." The man dropped his cigarette to the floor and crushed it with his heel. "I've worked on many movies, though, and I can tell you they always seem disorganized."

"Are you an actor?" Jessica asked.

The man laughed. "No. I'm just a lighting technician. Name's Harold Brooks. Ever heard of me?"

"Well, no—" Jessica began.

"That's OK. Sometimes my name appears in the credits at the very end of a movie, in very small letters." The old man laughed again. It wasn't a very nice laugh, Jessica decided. But she felt it was her duty as an extra to be polite to everyone, so she smiled.

"Do you know why they're putting fake bricks over the real bricks on the fireplace?" Elizabeth asked.

"See, in the bright lights we use for filming, those old bricks will look almost purple. We put those fakes over them so they'll look better on film." Mr. Brooks shook his head thoughtfully. "That's the movies for you. You can't tell the real from the fake." He frowned. "Or the facts from the lies."

"Twins!" Rolf called from across the ballroom. "Where *are* those twin creatures?"

Mr. Brooks nodded at the girls. "That would be you, ladies," he said, "if I don't miss my guess."

"Nice meeting you, Mr. Brooks," Jessica called, but he was already walking away.

"Hey, aren't you those famous movie stars?" a voice called as the twins turned the corner toward home late that afternoon.

Jessica looked up and saw a girl standing on the Wakefields' front lawn. "Look! Robin's here!" she cried, dashing across the street.

While Robin and Jessica hugged and screamed, Elizabeth hung back a little. "Aren't you glad to see me?" Robin asked, running over to hug Elizabeth.

"Don't mind her," Jessica said. "She's been a real space cadet all day."

"Of course I'm glad to see you, Robin," Elizabeth said. "I'm just a little tired, that's all."

"I guess being a movie star can really wear you out, huh?" Robin teased.

"Actually, *I'm* the one who'll be the real star," Jessica explained. "Elizabeth's just there as back-up."

"When did you get here, Robin?" Elizabeth asked as she opened the front door and headed inside.

"About an hour ago," Robin replied. "Your mom and dad picked me up at the bus station. Oh, and Steven, too." She shook her head. "He told really bad jokes all the way home."

"Sorry we couldn't be there to protect you," Jessica apologized.

"That's OK," Robin said. "I'd heard most of them before, so every time he got to the punchline, I'd yell it out before he had a chance." She grinned mischievously. "It was great."

"It's a shame you don't have a big brother, Robin," Jessica observed. "You could really make his life miserable."

The girls went upstairs to Jessica's room to unpack Robin's suitcase. "Tell me all about the movie," Robin urged. "Have you seen any stars? Did you get any autographs yet?"

"So far all we've done is get fitted for our costumes," Elizabeth admitted.

"Well, I'm still jealous," Robin said. "I can't believe you two are so lucky." She sucked in her checks and put on a sophisticated face. "Not when it's obvious that *I* am the true star."

Both twins laughed. "Actually, Shawn Brockaway is the star of this movie," Elizabeth pointed out.

"That's because nobody's seen *me* act yet," Jessica said.

Robin grinned at Elizabeth. "I can see Jessica hasn't changed a bit," she teased. "What's Shawn like, anyway?"

"We haven't even seen her yet," Jessica replied. "So far, all we've done is get yelled at by impatient wardrobe people."

"And we met that strange lighting technician," Elizabeth added.

"Big deal." Jessica fell onto her bed with a sigh.

"What's the movie about?" Robin asked.

"All we know is that it's a murder mystery about two girls our age. One dies and the other's the killer."

"Let me guess," Robin said. "You're the killer."

"Very funny," Jessica said. "The director gave me one page of script, and all I know is that I'm supposed to be someone named Luella who wants to eat cake."

"Ice cream," Elizabeth said automatically.

"*Cake,*" Jessica corrected. "I do know my lines."

"Well, they're supposed to be Elizabeth's lines too, aren't they?" Robin asked as she removed several T-shirts from her suitcase. "I mean, she could be the one who ends up doing the actual acting."

Jessica's eyes widened in horror. "I doubt *that's* going to happen. If it's her turn, I'm sure Elizabeth will just pretend to be me so I can do the actual acting."

"Fine by me," Elizabeth said quietly. "By the way, I think I may know something more about the movie."

"You do?" Jessica demanded. "Who told you?"

"No one. But I did some research in the library the other day so I'd be prepared for my interview with Becka." She looked over at Robin. "I'm doing a *Sixers* article on the director. Anyway, a long time ago, a girl named Lillian died at the mansion on her twelfth birthday. I think the movie is based on her death."

"Why didn't you tell me this before?" Jessica demanded, propping herself up on her elbows so she could glare at her sister.

Elizabeth shrugged. "I guess I forgot. I've been kind of preoccupied lately."

"You've been a total zomboid, if you ask me," Jessica grumbled.

"Anyway, that's all I really know. Lillian Keller had a fight with her cousin Hilda at her birthday party. Minutes later, Lillian was dead."

"The birthday party," Jessica said excitedly. "That's my scene! Lillian and Hilda are fighting and Luella—that's me—is trying to break it up."

"Either that, or Luella just likes ice cream," Elizabeth joked.

"It's cake," Jessica corrected her again.

"It's kind of a creepy story," Robin remarked. "I wonder how she died?"

"She fell from a balcony," Elizabeth replied. "Into the water. I guess—"

Suddenly Elizabeth fell silent. Something floated through her mind, a little wisp of memory she couldn't quite catch hold of. She strained, trying to remember, but it kept slipping away. Then she noticed her twin's face. Jessica had gone completely white.

"Jessica, what's the matter?" Elizabeth demanded in alarm.

"Nothing," Jessica whispered, shaking her head. "It's just—I thought I remembered something. I think it may just have been something I dreamed, though. I'm not sure."

"I've had that happen," Robin said. "It's like you can't be sure if it was real, or if it was something that only happened in a nightmare. Once I remembered being bitten by this huge dog. Then I realized it was just a nightmare I'd had a few days earlier."

Jessica seemed to relax a little. "You're right. I'm sure it was just a dream."

"Jessica, what did you think you were remembering?" Elizabeth asked tensely.

Jessica paused to consider. "I remembered something about falling," she answered slowly. "I was falling—"

"I've had falling dreams," Robin said.

"—and it was night," Jessica continued.

"—and there was lightning," Elizabeth added in a strained voice.

Jessica's eyes went wide. "And there was a box of jewels."

Elizabeth's felt a cold, sinking feeling deep in her stomach. "And Luella wanted ice cream," she whispered, "not cake."

It was just a coincidence, Elizabeth told herself for the hundredth time. Just a coincidence. That's what Robin had said.

Besides, maybe it was no big deal if identical twins had identical dreams. She and Jessica shared a special bond. They often experienced the same feelings and thoughts. And after all, they'd both been thinking about the movie a lot. It was only natural that they would dream about it too.

There was just one little problem with that theory. Jessica's dreams had started before she even knew what the movie was supposed to be about. *Before* she'd seen any of the script. That was difficult—maybe impossible—to explain.

Elizabeth glanced at the clock by her bed. Jessica and Robin were probably already asleep. Elizabeth wished that Robin was sleeping in her room tonight instead of Jessica's.

"What I need is something to distract me," Elizabeth muttered. She considered reading. That was her usual way to make herself sleepy. But then she thought of something much more interesting to do.

Elizabeth lifted the necklace out of her backpack and stared at it for a moment before setting it down on her desk. Then she twisted open the tube of glue she kept in her desk drawer and dabbed a little onto the back of the red stone. She glanced again at the letters engraved on the silver setting.

"Well, good-bye, *J.K.T.*, whoever you were," she said. She placed the stone over the letters and made sure it was firmly in place. Elizabeth sat the necklace down carefully on her nightstand and snapped off the light.

Seven

"The basic story of the movie involves the mysterious death of Lillian Keller," Becka explained.

It was Sunday afternoon, and Elizabeth finally had managed to corner Becka for an interview. They were sitting in two canvas-backed chairs in the ballroom. The fake bricks had all been put in place, and the painting completed. Nearby, Mr. Brooks and some other technicians were adjusting the huge, powerful lights overhead.

This morning Becka had given permission for Robin to hang out with Jessica on the set. Jessica was having her makeup applied now, along with the other extras, in preparation for the first scene they were going to shoot. Elizabeth had felt the tiniest twinge of jealousy that Jessica was going to get to act today, but, she reminded herself, she'd rather be interviewing Becka Silver.

Becka glanced over at Elizabeth's notepad. "Am I talking too fast for you?"

"Oh, no. Besides, if I miss something, I've got my recorder on too." Elizabeth pointed at the pocket-sized tape recorder she had borrowed from her father. This was the most important interview she'd ever done, and she didn't want to miss a word.

"So anyway," Becka continued, "this movie is about Lillian Keller's murder."

Elizabeth looked up sharply. "Murder? Are you sure it was a murder?"

Becka pursed her lips. "I guess I should start at the beginning. See, Lillian's cousin, Hilda Tomlinson, lived here at the mansion with the Kellers. Hilda's mom and Lillian's mom were sisters. Mr. and Mrs. Tomlinson were killed in an airplane crash when Hilda was eleven." Becka shrugged. "Planes weren't all that reliable back then. Anyway, after their death, Hilda went to live with Lillian and her family, and I guess it wasn't always a bed of roses, if you know what I mean. You know how kids are."

Elizabeth nodded. She already knew most of this from the research she had done in the library.

Becka leaned forward. "Anyway, here's where it starts getting juicy. The day of Lillian's twelfth birthday party, a huge fight breaks out between

Lillian and Hilda. Lillian runs up to her mother's room, only her mom isn't there. Hilda comes up right behind her, they fight some more, and boom!—Lillian's over the side of the balcony. Everyone else arrives a few seconds later and finds Hilda standing on the balcony, holding a piece of torn fabric from Lillian's dress."

Elizabeth shuddered. It was a terrible story— even more so because she had dreamed so much of it already. Still, those were just dreams, she told herself. Just dreams and nothing more.

She shifted uncomfortably in her chair. "So what happened to Hilda?"

"Well, the Keller family didn't want her thrown in jail or anything. After all, she was just a child. Besides, they wanted to avoid any hint of scandal. They decided to call the whole thing an accident, and sent Hilda to a hospital for disturbed children. And as far as anyone knows, Hilda was never heard from again. We assume she died."

Elizabeth made a quick calculation in her head. "But she wouldn't be *that* old now. It's possible that she could still be alive."

"True, but we looked for her for a long time and never found any trace of her. All we know is that she left the hospital when she turned eighteen, and then disappeared."

Elizabeth looked up from her notepad. "What a great mystery."

"Yep. It was quite a scandal at the time. Of

course, Mr. and Mrs. Keller are dead now, and this mansion has been closed up for decades, but lots of people still remember who the Kellers were. In their day, they were very influential. And *very* rich." Becka grinned. "You might even say disgustingly rich. What I wouldn't give to be that disgusting!" Suddenly she reached over and grabbed Elizabeth's pad. "You didn't write that down, did you?"

Elizabeth laughed. "Sure. It's a great quote."

Becka tossed the pad back. "Erase it, OK? It's bad for the image. Write down something about how money doesn't matter and I'm doing this because I've loved film since the day I was born." She paused, tapping her finger on her chin. "Now where were we?"

"Um, the Kellers. Were there any other kids?"

Becka shook her head. "Nope. Lillian was the last member of the Keller line."

"So how will we ever know for sure if Hilda really killed Lillian?"

"We won't," Becka said, wiggling her eyebrows. "Now do you see why this is such a great story for a movie?"

"Actually, Jon, I prefer a lighter shade of blush," Jessica said, gazing at her reflection in the mirror.

Jon, the makeup artist, rolled his eyes. "Honey, I was doing makeup for the movies when you were still learning to drool. Trust me on this."

"But this makes me look orange!" Jessica protested.

"It won't look that way on film. You have to remember that movie makeup isn't the same as your usual makeup."

Jessica scowled at her reflection. "If you say so," she said reluctantly.

"I do say so," Jon said firmly as he brushed her cheeks with the thick, dark powder.

Robin leaned against the mirror, her head cocked to one side. "I think it's really you, Jessica. Sort of a Bozo the Clown look with a little extra mascara."

Just then a harried-looking man stuck his head into the makeup room. "Everyone ready?" he demanded.

"Ready as they'll ever be," Jon said, putting the finishing touches on Jessica's face. "This is the last one."

"Come on, kid," the man said. "We need all extras on the set for the first part of the party scene."

Jessica and Robin hustled down the hall to the ballroom set. Becka and her assistants were already busy positioning the extras, moving them here and there like pieces of furniture. Maria and Mandy were sitting at a table with several other girls, all wearing old-fashioned dresses and covered with the same thick makeup. "Hey, Jessica!" Mandy called excitedly.

"You are *so* lucky," Robin said for the millionth

time. She gave Jessica a thumbs-up sign and headed over to the spot behind Becka's chair where Elizabeth and several other onlookers were sitting.

"Come on," a young woman urged, grabbing Jessica's arm and yanking her onto the set. The woman positioned Jessica behind a chair, leaning slightly forward.

"No, a little more to the left," Becka called out. The assistant moved Jessica to the side. She was still leaning over the chair, but in a slightly different direction. "We're getting a hot spot on her forehead," the cameraman called out.

Jon materialized instantly and pounded on Jessica's forehead with a powder puff. "Better?" he called out.

"Better," the cameraman replied.

"OK," Becka announced loudly. "All of you will need to remember exactly where you are right now. Keep your eyes focused in the direction we've told you to look. Do not look at the camera. Let me repeat that for those of you who may be a little dense. Do *not* look at the camera." Becka paused to mutter something over her shoulder to Murray, who nodded and dashed out of the room.

"Shawn Brockaway is going to come out so we can run through this scene," Becka continued. "You are not to talk to her, or ask for her autograph. Do you all understand?"

Jessica glanced over at Elizabeth, who was taking everything down on her notepad. Elizabeth gave her a little wave, but Jessica knew it would probably be unprofessional to wave back.

Suddenly there was a bustle of activity as several new people came onto the set. In the middle of the group was a petite redhaired girl.

"Shawn Brockaway," Mandy whispered.

"She looks smaller than she does on TV," Jessica whispered back.

Shawn walked directly to the seat in front of Jessica. "Excuse me," Shawn snapped. "Would you mind not breathing down my neck?"

"But this is where—" Jessica began.

"Just move back a few steps, Jasmine," Becka called out quickly.

"It's Jessica," Jessica said.

Shawn made a disgusted face. "Who on earth could possibly care *what* your name is? You're an extra!"

While Shawn flopped into the chair, an assistant ran forward to position Jessica in a new spot near Maria.

"A real sweetheart, isn't she?" Maria said under her breath.

Jessica felt a flush creeping into her face—not that anyone would ever see it under all the makeup. Shawn Brockaway had actually yelled at her, and for no reason!

"All right, Shawn, let's do a run-through," Becka called out. "It's real simple. You look down at the box, you read the card, you realize it's from your mother, you gaze in gratitude toward her, stage left. Then you give us the big Shawn Brockaway smile."

"Where exactly is this box I'm supposed to be looking at?" Shawn snapped.

Becka rolled her eyes. "Props! We need the box!"

A young woman came running over with a small gift-wrapped box with a large pink bow on top. She set the box on the table in front of Shawn.

"Don't make me wait again," Shawn griped at the prop woman. "I don't want to spend all day on this one stupid scene."

Jessica couldn't believe her ears. Shawn was actually yelling at a grown woman! And what's more, the woman was actually taking it!

"All right, let's see how it goes." Becka sounded tired. "Action."

From her new position, Jessica could just see the side of Shawn's face. But even from that angle, it was easy to see how Shawn's expression changed completely. Suddenly she transformed into a sweet, thoughtful girl.

Shawn looked down at the box and gingerly opened the card. She read for a moment, and then, with an expression brimming with gratitude, looked off to the left, exactly as if she were gazing lovingly at her mother. Actually, she was looking at a very fat sound technician with a cigar in his mouth.

"That's good," Becka said. "OK, now we'll do a

take. Listen up, extras. I know this is your first actual scene, but you only have to do one thing. Look at Lillian—which means look at Shawn—as if you can't wait to see what's in the box. When you see her look over at her mom, I want Maria and Jasmine to turn your heads and look in the same direction. All right?"

"And none of you had better mess up," Shawn added sharply.

"Quiet on the set!" the assistant director yelled.

Just then, a man ran in front of the camera carrying a little chalkboard with a a wooden strip on top which he snapped loudly. *Wow, just like the movies,* Jessica thought as the set grew still.

"And action!" Becka called.

Just as before, Shawn looked down at the box, read the card, and gazed lovingly off to one side. As Shawn looked away, Jessica turned her head in the same direction.

"Cut!" Becka said. "Perfect."

Maria leaned closer to Jessica. "See? That's why Shawn gets so much work. She's an incredible jerk, but she's also a really good actress. They call her 'one-shot Shawn' because she almost always gets it right the first time. Some actors need ten or fifteen takes to get it."

"You're right about the incredible jerk part, that's for sure," Jessica whispered as she watched Shawn stalk off to her dressing room.

"OK, extras, that's it for today," Becka called.

"Good job. Back here tomorrow for more. Don't be late!"

"That's it?" Jessica asked Maria. "I thought this was supposed to be a whole party. That was only ten seconds."

"That's the way it works. Movies aren't made in the same order as you see them on the screen. They're made with a scene here and a scene there, and then later, the director and the editors put the whole thing together like a puzzle."

"That seems kind of dumb."

"Not really. See, the next part of the party they show might be a long shot—a scene where they're showing the whole room. Well, for that, the lights and cameras will have to be moved around. While that's going on, Becka will head to a different set that's already been prepared. Right now they're probably going off to Lillian's bedroom to do a scene in there."

"So we'll never even know what's going on in this movie until we see it in the theater?" Jessica asked.

"That's right," Maria confirmed. "Unless you read the script, you'll never really get the whole picture."

"How are my little movie stars?" Mrs. Wakefield asked as Jessica, Elizabeth, and Robin trooped into the Wakefields' living room that afternoon.

"Great!" Robin cried. "I got hired too!"

"You did? How did that happen?" Mrs. Wake-field asked.

Robin shrugged. "My great natural beauty, of course."

"Plus the fact that one of the extras quit," Eliza-beth added wryly.

"Why would someone quit?"

"Shawn Brockaway, that's why," Jessica said. "Shawn bullied a poor extra until she couldn't stand it anymore."

Elizabeth nodded. "I was with Becka when the girl quit. She said she'd strangle Shawn if she had to spend another minute with her."

Mrs. Wakefield laughed. "Shawn can't be *that* bad."

"Yes, she can, Mom," Jessica said. "And she defi-nitely is."

"Well, I can handle Shawn Brockaway," Robin said confidently. "She doesn't worry me."

"What I can't stand is that I don't even know what's going on in this dumb movie," Jessica com-plained. "All we did today is sit there while Shawn looked at a box."

"Well, fortunately, while you were pretending to be an actor, I was interviewing Becka," Elizabeth said. "And she gave me a copy of the complete script."

"Great! Why don't you read it and tell me what happens?"

"That's what I'm going upstairs to do right

now," Elizabeth said. She couldn't wait to see how Lillian's story unfolded.

"You know, I don't even need to know the *whole* story," Robin added. "I just want to know one thing."

"What's that?" Elizabeth asked.

Robin threw up her hands in exasperation. "We never saw what was in the box—the one that Shawn was making such a big deal about opening. What was in that box?"

Eight

◇

"You'd better grab the bathroom quick before Jessica gets in there," Elizabeth advised Robin that evening as the girls were getting ready for bed.

"I think her new stardom may be going to her head," Robin said with a grin. "Last night I was afraid we'd have to have her surgically removed from the mirror."

Robin dashed into the bathroom and shut the door. Then Elizabeth hurried over to her bed and reached under her pillow for the necklace.

She held it up and gazed at it. The stones flashed and sparkled in the light. Half the necklace was clean now, and its strange beauty had grown even more entrancing. Elizabeth figured that she must have sneaked into her room at least a dozen times that evening to look at it. Even earlier in the day, while she'd been on the busy movie set interviewing Becka, Elizabeth had found her mind returning again and again to the necklace.

It's strange, Elizabeth thought. *Once I had the necklace, Jessica never even asked about it again.* It had seemed so important to Jessica when she'd first found it, and now it was as if she had completely forgotten about it.

"What's that?" Robin asked as she emerged suddenly from the bathroom.

Elizabeth closed her hand over the necklace, but she knew it was too late. "What?" she asked innocently.

"That. In your hand."

Reluctantly Elizabeth opened her fingers.

Robin gasped. "Is that a necklace?"

Elizabeth nodded. "It's just costume jewelry. You know— fake stones."

"It's amazing," Robin said, her eyes wide. "I mean, it looks like it could be worth a fortune. Where did you get it?"

"I found it on the beach. In the surf. Well, actually, Jessica found it, but she gave it to me."

"Jessica *gave* you this?" Robin looked amazed. She held out her hand. "Let me see it."

"It's still kind of dirty," Elizabeth said, clutching the necklace a little tighter. "I haven't gotten it completely cleaned up yet."

"I can see that. Let me look at it."

"No!" Elizabeth said so sharply that Robin jumped back in surprise.

"What's the matter with you?" Robin cried. "I wasn't going to steal it or anything!"

Elizabeth managed a weak smile. "I know. Sorry," she said more calmly. "It's just that it's kind of fragile, that's all." She slipped the necklace under her pillow.

Robin gave her a strange look. "You know, Elizabeth, you've really been acting weird lately. Are you sure you haven't had a personality transplant since the last time I saw you?"

Elizabeth laughed uncomfortably. "Not that I remember." But she knew Robin had a point. Why would she have yelled at her cousin over a piece of jewelry? That wasn't like her at all.

Elizabeth climbed into bed with a sigh. "I'm sorry if I've been a little distracted, Robin. I've got a lot on my mind, like the movie, and the story I have to write about Becka. Plus, I haven't been sleeping all that well."

"You haven't started snoring, have you?" Robin asked suspiciously. She slid into the sleeping bag she'd placed on the floor next to Elizabeth's bed.

"I wish," Elizabeth said. "I'd rather be snoring than having weird nightmares."

Robin smiled sympathetically. "Well, look on the bright side. Jessica said she's stopped having those falling nightmares. You'll probably stop having yours soon too."

"I hope you're right," Elizabeth replied, sighing. "Will it bother you if I leave the light on by my bed for a few minutes? I want to read some more of this script before I go to sleep."

Robin waved her hand. "Trust me, I'm beat. Right now, nothing could keep me awake."

Within minutes Robin was snoring lightly. *Great, and she was worried I might snore,* Elizabeth thought ruefully.

She opened the script and began to read.

"My mother always said I would get it," Hilda *wailed. "It should be mine, not yours."*

"I don't care," Lillian *shot back, pushing away an enormous piece of birthday cake. "My mother gave it to me. She would never give me something that wasn't hers to give!"*

"I'm not going to let you keep it, Lillian," Hilda *said with grim determination. "I don't care what I have to do."*

"Are you threatening me?" Lillian *demanded.*

Hilda didn't answer, but her eyes blazed in response.

"I'm taking this straight upstairs to put it in Mother's jewelry box," Lillian *said. "Where you can't get at it."*

"But it was my mother's," Hilda *cried.*

Lillian ran out the door. Behind her, she could hear Luella call, "Don't run off! There's ice cream!"

She ran up the winding staircase. By the time she reached her mother's bedroom, she was panting. The door to the room was open just an inch or two. Lillian threw it open and dashed in, trying to hold back a flood of tears. She and Hilda argued frequently, but this had been their worst fight ever.

Lillian heard a noise and turned. She could barely see through the tears that were welling up in her eyes. She wiped her eyes and her gaze fell on her mother's box of jewels—and the hand that was plunging into them.

Suddenly she was outside. She felt the wind on her face. The air was cold and damp. Black storm clouds raced overhead. As lightning sliced through the sky, Lillian felt the railing behind her. Cold fear gripped her, but she couldn't back up any farther. A hand was coming toward her. All she could see was that hand—that horrible hand. Her shoes slipped on the damp balcony, and she began to fall.

Even as she fell, the hand reached for her throat.

Lillian felt a tug, and something scraped against the flesh of her throat.

She screamed as the jagged black rocks rushed to meet her. Lightning tore through the clouds again and she could see a dark, shadowed face watching from the balcony above her.

Then she saw the hand—the hand with only four fingers. And entwined in those fingers was her necklace, glittering in the eerie blue glow of the lightning.

Elizabeth awoke with every nerve in her body tingling. She felt as if she had been electrified.

"Are you OK?" Robin's frightened voice came

from the dark. "I heard you crying in your sleep."

Elizabeth reached over and snapped on the light. Her hands were trembling. "I was there," she whispered. "I was Lillian. In my dream I was Lillian. I was falling over the railing. I could feel it all, Robin."

"Maybe you shouldn't be reading that script right before you go to sleep," Robin said.

Elizabeth hesitated. *Maybe it was just the script. Maybe the entire nightmare was just a replay of the script.* "But it seemed so real," she said at last.

"Nightmares can seem awfully real," Robin assured her. "Until you wake up, that is."

"I guess you're right," Elizabeth agreed slowly. She hugged her knees to her chest and tried to stop shivering. "Some of the details are already starting to fade."

"That's normal. I can never remember my dreams very clearly."

Elizabeth glanced at the script on her nightstand. Then she turned off the light and leaned back against her pillow. "Sorry I woke you up."

"No problem. I hope you don't have another nightmare."

Elizabeth lay in the dark, trying to remember parts of the dream, but the memories kept slipping away. She rolled over and reached her hand under her pillow. Her fingers touched the necklace.

The necklace!

That's what Mrs. Keller had given Lillian for her

birthday—a necklace! Suddenly the entire dream came rushing back into Elizabeth's mind. She remembered the look on Hilda's face as she insisted that the necklace had belonged to her dead mother. Elizabeth clutched at her throat. Once again, she felt the sensation of the necklace being snatched away as she fell backward from the balcony. She could see the beautiful necklace shimmering in the glow of the lightning—the smooth silver settings and the polished stones, the huge, glittering, impossibly large ruby.

"The necklace," Elizabeth whispered aloud.

"Jessica, wake up," Elizabeth whispered, snapping on the light in her twin's bedroom.

"Come back in the morning," Jessica mumbled.

"It's really important," Elizabeth said. "Please."

Robin appeared in the doorway. "What's going on?"

"It's the necklace, Robin," Elizabeth burst out. "It's the same necklace. The necklace Lillian died for."

Robin and Jessica exchanged confused looks.

"Come on," Elizabeth urged as she led the way back to her room. "I'll explain everything."

"This had better be good," Jessica grumbled as she and Robin flopped down onto Elizabeth's bed. "I was dreaming that I was the youngest person ever to win the best-actress Oscar. I was just starting my acceptance speech: First, I want to thank all the little people—"

"Jessica," Elizabeth interrupted. "This is serious." She reached under her pillow and pulled out the necklace, setting it down on the comforter in front of her. "Remember when you wanted to know what was in the box that Lillian was about to open, Robin? Well, it was a necklace."

"So?" Robin asked, yawning.

"So how do I know that?" Elizabeth asked.

"You read the script," Robin replied.

Elizabeth shook her head. She reached for the script and handed it to Robin. "I used a paper clip to mark the place where I stopped reading. The party scene comes late in the story. I haven't read that part yet. I swear I never saw anything about a necklace in there."

Elizabeth looked over at Jessica, who was staring intently at the necklace. Suddenly Jessica looked up, and their eyes met.

"You sensed it too, didn't you, Jess?" Elizabeth asked softly.

Jessica barely nodded her head. "For some reason I wanted the necklace around. I felt as if I *needed* it. Then, when you finally took it away from me, I felt—well, I actually felt relieved."

Robin stared from Elizabeth to Jessica and back again. "I don't know what you two are talking about, but I skimmed the part you read, Elizabeth," she said. "And there's nothing about a necklace."

"Keep reading," Elizabeth urged. "Read the party scene."

Elizabeth and Jessica watched as Robin's eyes scanned several pages. Then she gasped. "Here it is," she said. "It's part of the stage directions. *The box contains a platinum necklace, highlighted by a single large ruby.*"

All three girls dropped their gaze to the necklace.

Robin gulped. "You're *sure* you didn't read that part last night?"

Elizabeth shook her head. "Jess, have you had any more bad dreams since you gave me the necklace?"

"No. Not one."

"Did you ever dream about a hand? A strange hand with—"

"—with only four fingers?" Jessica said, her voice shaking.

"OK, now I *definitely* have the creeps," Robin said

"What do you think all this means, Elizabeth?" Jessica asked softly.

Elizabeth shook her head. "I don't know. If I say what I'm thinking, you'll both say I'm nuts."

Jessica smiled slightly. "Try us."

"Well," Elizabeth began, "Lillian got a gift that Hilda thought should have been hers. A necklace. I think that when Lillian fell from the balcony, someone grabbed the necklace from around her neck. But maybe the person who did it couldn't hold on to it. Maybe the necklace fell along with Lillian onto the rocks and was washed out to sea."

Jessica nodded. "And if it was washed out to sea, it would get slowly covered by barnacles and sediment and dirt. And it would be lost forever."

"Unless it happened to wash ashore, only a few hundred feet from the Keller mansion."

"You two *are* nuts," Robin said. "Do you know how big a coincidence it would be for that very same necklace to suddenly wash ashore just as they're getting ready to make a movie about it?"

"You're right," Elizabeth agreed. "Except that maybe it wasn't a coincidence. Just like maybe the dreams aren't a coincidence. Maybe someone is trying to tell us something."

"Right," Robin said doubtfully. "And who could possibly have raised the necklace up off the ocean bottom and practically delivered it into your hands?"

"Only one person I can think of," Jessica said hoarsely.

Elizabeth looked over and saw her own fear reflected in Jessica's eyes.

"Lillian," she whispered.

Nine

"I think it's time for an experiment," Elizabeth announced to Jessica and Robin early Monday morning.

"Can we talk about it downstairs?" Jessica asked as she ran a brush through her hair. "I'm starving. I want some breakfast."

"Do you really want to discuss this in front of Mom, Dad, and Steven?" Elizabeth demanded.

"Good point."

Robin stopped rolling up her sleeping bag. "So what's the experiment, Elizabeth?"

"Well," Elizabeth began, "our theory is that the necklace Jessica found belonged to Lillian, right?"

"Right," Robin said.

"We also suspect that the necklace is somehow responsible for the nightmares about Lillian that Jessica and I have been having. Right?"

"Right," Jessica said. "When you have the necklace, you have the nightmares."

"Well, we should test out our theory," Elizabeth said.

"How?" Jessica asked.

"We should have someone new keep the necklace for a while, to see if that person has the same nightmares."

"Who would want to do that?" Robin said with a laugh.

Elizabeth and Jessica looked at each other, then turned to stare at Robin.

Robin's mouth fell open. "No way. I hate nightmares."

"Come on, Robin. There's no other way to be sure," Elizabeth coaxed. As much as she hated to put her cousin through the terror she'd experienced, it seemed like the only solution.

Robin made a face. "I thought this visit was going to be fun," she grumbled. "Now I'm supposed to volunteer to have nightmares about a dead girl."

"Does that mean you'll do it?" Jessica asked.

Robin held up her index finger. "One night and that's it," she said.

Elizabeth opened her dresser drawer, where she'd hidden the necklace last night. She held the necklace in her hand for a moment. "Maybe we shouldn't do this," she said.

"Elizabeth," Jessica said firmly, "give the necklace to Robin."

Elizabeth took a deep breath. "You're right. But even now, suspecting what I do, it's so hard to let go of it."

"Don't forget," Jessica said grimly, "if our theory is right, one person has already been killed over this necklace."

Slowly Elizabeth passed the necklace to Robin. The simple gesture seemed to take all her willpower.

"It *is* awfully pretty, isn't it?" Robin asked as she examined the smooth red stone in the middle. She held the necklace up to her neck and struck a pose. "What do you think, guys?" she asked with a grin.

"I think you'd better be very careful," Elizabeth warned.

"OK now, which one are you—Jasmine or Elizabeth?" Becka asked when the girls arrived at the mansion that morning.

"I'm Elizabeth," Elizabeth said, suppressing a grin.

"And I'm *Jessica*," Jessica muttered.

"Right." Becka nodded. "Elizabeth, do you want to hang around with me today, or take your turn acting?"

"Actually, I'd rather follow you some more, if that's all right," Elizabeth said.

"Great," Becka said, sounding pleased. She turned to Robin. "And you're the girl who's filling in for the extra Shawn scared off, right?" she asked.

Robin nodded. "Now don't you get scared off too, all right? We're getting into scenes where it's important that we have the same extras every day."

"Shawn Brockaway doesn't scare me," Robin said.

"Good for you," Becka said with a sigh, "because she sure scares me."

Jessica and Robin headed toward the wardrobe trailer while Becka huddled with several of her assistants. Elizabeth figured she'd try to stay out of the way. Now that she'd read the script, she had a feeling she would be able to understand the moviemaking process better. *Of course,* she thought wryly, *it also helps that I recognizee several of the sets from my very own dreams.*

She wandered over to the winding staircase that led upstairs. She had never been up those stairs, but she felt certain that she knew exactly where Mrs. Keller's bedroom was—upstairs, down the hall, and on the left.

Elizabeth glanced over at Becka. She was still deep in conversation. Almost without thinking, Elizabeth started up the stairs.

These are the stairs Lillian ran up, she told herself. *At least that's the way it was in my dream.*

She ascended slowly, taking the steps one at a time. Soon she was at the top, gazing down a long hallway. *It's that door over there,* she thought. *That's Mrs. Keller's room.*

Elizabeth crept down the hallway, looking over

her shoulder anxiously. She could tell that the workmen had been there recently. There were boards leaning on sawhorses, and a canvas drop-cloth covered the floor. Luckily, no one else was there now. The cameras, lights, and all the hustle and bustle downstairs seemed a million miles away.

At the doorway to Mrs. Keller's bedroom, Elizabeth paused and swallowed the lump in her throat. Her hand was cold and damp on the doorknob. *This is impossible,* she told herself. *I've never been here before, and yet it's completely familiar.*

Elizabeth eased open the door a crack. She took a deep breath, trying to slow her pounding heart.

Then she heard the noise. It was very faint, the kind of sound that might have come from the set downstairs. But it also could have been footsteps in the bedroom.

Just like in the dream! Elizabeth realized with a jolt. The memory was clear now—Lillian had heard someone in her mother's room. But whom? It couldn't have been Hilda. Lillian had come upstairs, leaving Hilda behind. There was no way Hilda could have gotten up here first. Was there?

Maybe Lillian's mother had made the sound. It was her bedroom, after all. Still, it was more likely that Mrs. Keller would have been downstairs at the party. And if she *had* been upstairs, she should have been able save her daughter from falling.

Elizabeth heard the noise again.

Come on, Elizabeth. You know you have to look in there, she told herself.

She pushed the door open a little wider. It swung back silently on its hinges. She already knew what she would see when she stepped into the room. There would be a large oak four-poster bed with a canopy.

And there it was. The very same bed.

She knew that she would see a large bureau against the opposite wall of the room, and there it was too, just as it had appeared in her dreams.

And she knew that the balcony would be off to the right.

Elizabeth crept forward on tiptoes, barely breathing.

"What are you doing here?"

Elizabeth jumped. "Mr. Brooks!"

The old man was standing on the balcony, his hands shoved deep into his pockets. He stepped into the room, staring at Elizabeth suspiciously. "What are you doing here?" he repeated.

"Just looking around," Elizabeth said in a small voice.

"You shouldn't be up here."

"I guess you're right. I just wanted to . . . um . . . see what the rest of the house was like."

Mr. Brooks seemed to relax a little. "I'm only concerned because there might be cables and things lying around. I wouldn't want you to get hurt."

"Are you setting up lights in here?"

The old man's expression darkened. "No, not yet," he said after a moment's hesitation. He reached into his shirt pocket with his right hand and pulled out a pack of cigarettes. "Actually, I came up here for a smoke. All those Hollywood types downstairs hate to be around cigarette smoke." He shrugged. "Terrible habit. I'm trying to quit."

Elizabeth watched as Mr. Brooks struggled to open the pack with one hand. *That's odd*, she thought, but just as she was about to offer to help, he managed to get it open.

"I guess I'd better head back downstairs," she said.

"Yes. That would be best."

Elizabeth turned and hurried out of the room and down the stairs. She breathed a deep sigh of relief as soon as she found herself back in the bright, noisy world on the first floor.

Elizabeth found Becka on the main ballroom set, arranging the extras and preparing for the next scene. This scene would be Jessica's big moment, when Luella would tell Lillian not to run off because they were going to cut the cake.

Of course, Elizabeth reminded herself, it wasn't cake Luella had wanted, it was ice cream. At least that's how it had been in her dream.

She shook her head. All these dreams and scripts and stories were enough to drive her crazy. What was the truth?

"Where'd you wander off to?" Becka asked Elizabeth absentmindedly.

"Oh, I was just looking around."

"Well, you're lucky. You missed Shawn's first explosion of the day. Someone forgot to get her favorite brand of diet soda. Naturally, she won't work until we get some." Becka sighed and reached into her purse. She pulled out a cigarette and gave Elizabeth an embarrassed smile. "I know, I know—they're bad for me. I've cut down to two or three a day. As soon as this movie's over, I'm going to stop cold turkey, cross my heart."

"I'm never going to touch one of those," Elizabeth said with a scowl.

"Good thing. You're a lot smarter than I am," Becka said. She stared at the unlit cigarette and sighed. Then she stuffed it back into her cigarette case and gave Elizabeth a grateful smile. "If I had you around twenty-four hours a day, Elizabeth, I just might manage to quit."

Suddenly something occurred to Elizabeth. She glanced around the set. Most of the people weren't smoking, but two or three were, including one of the lighting technicians. No one seemed to mind.

So why had Mr. Brooks said he had to sneak away upstairs to smoke?

"Diet soda?" Jessica asked in disbelief. "She won't work because they have the wrong brand of diet soda?"

"Sounds nutty, doesn't it?" Maria said. "But that's what I heard. We're all standing around here with nothing to do because Shawn won't come on the set until she gets *her* brand of soda."

"You weren't like that, were you?" Robin asked Maria. "I mean, when you were a big star?"

"Robin!" Jessica exclaimed. "Maria still is a star."

Maria shook her head ruefully. "No, I'm not, Jessica. And most of the time I'm glad I'm not. Being a star can make you do strange things—like refuse to work because of diet soda."

"You mean you did stuff like that?" Mandy asked doubtfully.

Maria shrugged. "I was no Shawn Brockaway, but I could get cranky sometimes."

"Well, what do we do now?" Jessica asked.

"Just hang out here on the set, until Becka says otherwise," Maria said.

Jessica rolled her eyes. How could Shawn keep them all waiting like this? Today was Jessica's big day. She'd practiced her lines at least a thousand times the day before, to make sure they'd be absolutely perfect.

"Hey, you two. This is supposed to be a party!" Jessica recited. She turned to Robin. "How was that?"

Robin sighed. "For the millionth time, it was fine. Superb. Brilliant."

"Wait! We still haven't cut the cake!" Jessica exclaimed. She shook her head. "It still isn't quite right. Maybe if I understood my motivation better . . ."

"Your motivation is that you're a pig," Mandy replied. "Now relax, will you?"

"There *is* such a thing as rehearsing too much," Maria pointed out gently.

"And there's definitely such a thing as hearing that line too much," Mandy added.

Jessica frowned. "Fine. I'll just go find something else to amuse myself with."

She stomped away, but since she had to stay on the set, she couldn't go very far. To kill time, she glanced over some of the old-fashioned things that had been placed around the set—old books, a china tea set, and framed pictures that were supposed to be of Lillian's family. One picture, of a young Mrs. Keller in her wedding gown, caught her attention. *Looks about the same as wedding gowns nowadays,* Jessica thought. *I guess some styles don't change all that much.*

Jessica looked up from the photo just in time to see Shawn appear on the set, smiling contentedly. "Everyone ready?" she asked casually.

"Did you get your soda?" Maria inquired sarcastically.

Shawn gave her a nasty grin. "You're not the star of *this* movie, Maria. I am. You wait for me, and that's just the way it is. Don't blame me because you're washed up as an actor."

Jessica could tell Maria was struggling to control

herself. Fortunately, Becka interrupted just in time, calling for everyone's attention.

"For some of you extras, this is going to be a little more complicated than yesterday's scene," she began. "Jasmine, you have two lines in this scene. Do you know them?"

"Backward and forward," Jessica said. "Maria helped make sure I was saying them right."

"Excellent. I'm sure you'll do fine. Thank you, Maria. You've always been one of the most talented young actors around." Becka looked pointedly at Shawn. "Not to mention being very professional and easy to work with."

Elizabeth sat on the edge of the set near Becka, waiting for Jessica's motion-picture debut.

While she was waiting, Elizabeth strained to get a better look at the necklace Shawn was wearing for the scene. It was silver—or platinum—and covered with gleaming stones, but it was nothing like the necklace Jessica had found on the beach.

"How do you know that's what Lillian's necklace really looked like?" Elizabeth asked Becka.

Becka shrugged. "We don't. That's just our best guess, based on newspaper accounts and stuff like that. We had it specially made. Not bad, huh?"

Elizabeth nodded. *Not bad, but not right, either,* she thought to herself.

"A little less light on the girl on the end," Becka yelled. "That costume is bright enough as it is."

Elizabeth saw a technician hurry over to adjust one of the lights. It was Mr. Brooks. He reached up with both hands and tilted the light downward just a few inches. Then he stood casually, hands in his pockets, awaiting further instructions.

Elizabeth furrowed her brow. It was odd, but she had the strange sense that she had just missed something. She strained to remember what it was, but the thought slipped away. She was left with nothing but a lingering, uneasy feeling—a feeling that had something to do with Mr. Brooks.

Ten

"Action!"

Jessica stood waiting, listening word by word, syllable by syllable. Shawn and Ashley Korman, the actress playing Hilda, were facing each other. As soon as Ashley said the word *parties*, it would be time for Jessica to say her first line.

"My mother would never give me something that didn't rightly belong to her," Shawn said fiercely.

"But she has," Ashley fired back even more vehemently. "I know. I've seen it many times before—around her neck when she went out to parties."

There it is, Jessica thought. *My cue.*

"Hey, you two!" she called out. "This is supposed to be a party!"

Instantly Jessica was sure she had messed up.

Her voice had been much too high—she'd sounded like some kind of cartoon mouse. Had she even said the right words?

Jessica gazed around the set carefully. To her complete amazement, the scene was still going on. No one had yelled *cut*. Was it possible that she'd actually been OK?

Shawn, in her role as Lillian, was still speaking spitefully. "You're lying because you're jealous, Hilda," she said. "It's mine. My mother gave it to me."

"But it belonged to my mother. My mother!" Ashley.

With a jolt, Jessica realized that her second line was coming up in a few seconds. As soon as Shawn started to run away, it would be time.

"You're being awful. I hate you!" Shawn screamed. She turned, and Jessica was surprised to see that she had actual tears in her eyes. Shawn rubbed a hand across her face and ran toward the side of the set.

"Wait!" Jessica cried. "Don't run off! There's ice cream!"

Next to her, Elizabeth heard Becka groan. "Cut!" she yelled.

Jessica looked confused for a moment, and then crestfallen.

"Where did she get *ice cream* from?" Becka asked no one in particular.

Elizabeth met Jessica's eyes. Elizabeth knew exactly where her twin had gotten *ice cream*. It was what Luella had said in the dream—ice cream, not cake.

"Are you kidding me?" Shawn shrieked. "We lose that take because of a stupid extra?"

"Calm down, Shawn," Becka said soothingly, as Jessica's face flamed red.

"*You* calm down. That was a great take! I was perfect! I had major tears going! Now I have to do it again because of this little airhead?"

Elizabeth had to bite her tongue to keep from rising to her sister's defense, but she knew Jessica was already embarrassed enough. The last thing Elizabeth wanted to do was make things worse.

"Shawn, just calm down," Becka said. "We're going to take the scene again."

Shawn shot Jessica a menacing look. Elizabeth had never seen Jessica look more devastated. She was relieved when Maria whispered something into Jessica's ear, and her twin seemed to recover her composure a little.

On the next take, Jessica got her lines right, but Ashley Korman forgot one of hers. Shawn exploded again. *At least this time she didn't pick on Jessica*, Elizabeth thought with relief.

On take three, everything seemed to be going fine until one of the sound technicians dropped a microphone so low it nearly knocked Shawn on the head. Naturally, Shawn spent the next five minutes screaming at the crew.

Finally, on take four, Becka was able to say, "All right, print that one."

"Did you hear what I said?" Jessica hissed, running over to Elizabeth. "It was because of those stupid dreams! My acting career could be ruined. I can't believe I got that line wrong. I ruined the scene."

"Actually, Jess," Elizabeth said, trying to sound comforting, "no one else may have known it, but you got the line *right*."

That night, Jessica was awakened from a sound sleep by the sound of terrified screams. After a second of sleepy confusion, she realized that it was Robin. Jessica turned on the light and leaped out of bed.

"Wake up! Wake up!" she cried, shaking Robin by the shoulders.

"NO! NO! Aaaah!" Robin screamed, thrashing around in her sleep.

"Robin, wake up!" Jessica dashed into the bathroom and came back with a glass of water.

"What are you doing?" Elizabeth demanded, rushing into Jessica's room. "What's going on?"

"We have to get her up," Jessica exclaimed, "before she wakes up the whole house!" She launched the water at Robin's face.

"Hey!" Robin sat up in her sleeping bag, blinking and wiping her face.

"I had to wake you up," Jessica said apologetically. "You were having a nightmare."

Robin shivered and began fumbling with the neck of her nightgown. "I know. It was horrible!"

As Elizabeth watched, Robin pulled the necklace out from under the collar of her nightgown.

"You *wore* it?" Jessica gasped.

"What was I supposed to do with it? Eat it? It's a necklace."

Jessica shook her head. "We should have warned you. I just slept with it under my pillow and I had nightmares."

"Maybe that's why you couldn't wake up as easily, Robin," Elizabeth suggested. "You had the necklace closer to you."

"Well, I want to keep it as far away from me as possible from now on," Robin said emphatically. "Here, take it back!" She undid the clasp and held the necklace out to Elizabeth. But just as Elizabeth reached for it, Robin snatched it back.

Elizabeth exchanged glances with Jessica. "You'd better just set it down on the dresser, Robin," she suggested gently.

Robin shrugged. "Why don't I just hang on to it?" she said.

"A second ago you wanted to get rid of it," Elizabeth pointed out.

Robin's eyes clouded. "I did, didn't I?"

"Once you give it away, you'll feel better," Jessica said. "I know I did."

"I think there's something about that necklace that makes you want to hang on to it," Elizabeth said.

"When I had it, I couldn't seem to think about much of anything else." She looked away as she felt herself blushing. "I even sneaked into the science lab at school to get a solvent so I could clean it off."

"I got more of it cleaned up this evening," Robin said proudly. "Even the clasp."

"Robin." Elizabeth's voice was firm. "Put the necklace down."

"Why should I?" Robin demanded.

Jessica got up and headed for the bathroom.

Why is she running off right now, when I need her to help me with Robin? Elizabeth wondered. She turned her attention back to Robin. "Come on, Robin. Just put it down and you'll feel—"

Suddenly Jessica reappeared, carrying another glass of water again. Without a word, she let it fly. The water caught Robin with her mouth open. While she was sputtering, Jessica reached down and snatched the necklace out of her hand. She tossed it onto the bed as if it were a dangerous snake.

"Would you stop it with the water already?" Robin cried.

Jessica smiled at Elizabeth. "I think she'll be fine in a minute."

"Are you ready to tell us about the nightmare, Robin?" Elizabeth asked a few minutes later, when Robin seemed to be back to normal.

Robin bit her lip. "I . . . I was falling. I remember that part."

"And the sky was dark overhead," Jessica chimed in.

"With jagged bolts of lightning," Elizabeth added.

The three girls exchanged a nervous look.

"There was a box of jewels, all shiny and beautiful," Robin began again.

"And a hand digging into the box," Jessica said softly.

Elizabeth took a deep breath. "A hand with only four fingers," she concluded. Her cousin's shocked expression told her all that she needed to know. Robin had had the same dream as the twins.

"OK," Robin joked shakily, "I'm ready to go home to San Diego now."

Elizabeth reached over and gave Robin a hug. "Do you remember wearing a necklace in the dream?" she asked.

"Yes." Robin extended a shaky finger toward the bed. "*That* necklace."

"And did someone tear it away from your neck just as you were falling?" Jessica asked in a whisper.

"Yes."

"Was it the four-fingered hand that tore the necklace away?" Elizabeth pursued.

"Yes. Yes, but then he dropped it."

"Who?" Elizabeth demanded.

"The man with the four-fingered hand," Robin whispered.

"What makes you think it was a man?" Elizabeth asked. "I could never see a face."

"It was a man," Robin said. "I saw him."

"As you were falling?" Jessica asked.

"No. Standing over the box of jewels. He was digging his hand into the box and I . . . I mean *Lillian* . . . came in. He looked right at her. He was—" Robin shivered. "He was angry. Then his expression changed. He wasn't angry anymore. Just determined."

Elizabeth looked at Jessica. "I never saw any of that."

Jessica shook her head. "Neither did I."

"I saw Hilda, too," Robin said.

"Me too," Jessica said. "When she was arguing with Lillian."

"No, that's not what I mean," Robin said shakily. "I saw that part too, almost exactly like the scene we did for the movie except—except that you were right, Jessica. Luella wanted ice cream, not cake." She took a deep breath. "But then later I saw Hilda again."

"After the party?" Elizabeth asked.

"Definitely. I know the party was over, because I—I mean Lillian—had fallen off the balcony. She was hanging there by her fingertips. She looked up and saw Hilda standing there, staring down at her as she—" Suddenly Robin's throat seemed go dry. "Hilda was the last person Lillian saw before she . . . before she died."

Eleven

"You know what I think?" Elizabeth said as the girls gathered around the breakfast table on Tuesday morning. "I think we've been having these nightmares for a reason." She glanced over her shoulder to make sure her parents weren't within earshot. "I think Lillian *wants* us to be having them."

Jessica rubbed her eyes wearily. "There's just one problem with that theory, Elizabeth. Lillian's dead."

"Who's dead?"

The girls turned around to see Steven saunter into the kitchen and head straight for the refrigerator.

"Nobody's dead," Elizabeth said quickly.

"Then who's this Lillian person?" Steven asked as he pulled out half a chocolate cake.

"She's a person in the movie we're making," Jessica explained. "She was real, but now she's just an actress."

"Ah." Steven nodded. "Thanks for *not* clearing that up, Jessica."

"Are you really going to eat a piece of cake for breakfast?" Robin asked, her eyes wide.

"Of course not," Steven said as he grabbed a fork and joined them at the table. "I'm going to eat the whole thing."

"He's not kidding, either," Jessica muttered.

"So anyway, this Lillian girl is dead, right?" Steven asked.

"What do you care?" Jessica asked irritably.

"I'm just making conversation," Steven said. "So how did she croak?"

"She fell off a balcony," Robin replied.

"Bummer," Steven said, his mouth full of cake.

"Close your mouth, Steven," Elizabeth advised. "Robin's got a weak stomach."

"How did she fall? Did somebody push her, or what?" Steven asked.

"We're not sure," Robin replied.

"You guys, maybe we should go *upstairs* and talk," Elizabeth said pointedly. If they wound up telling Steven too much, she knew they'd regret it later.

"Hey, I can take a hint," Steven said, pushing back his chair. "You've got big heads now that you're actresses. Fine. See if *I* go see your movie."

He grabbed his cake and headed for the family room. "And by the way, I can tell you right now who killed Lillian."

"You can?" Robin asked hopefully.

"Sure. The butler did it. It's always that way in movies."

"We've got to watch what we say around people," Elizabeth whispered when the three girls were gathered in her room later that morning. "We don't want everyone to start thinking we're crazy."

"Maybe we are," Jessica said.

Elizabeth shook her head. "Think about it. All our nightmares were about the same thing — Lillian's last few minutes of life. It's almost as if she wants whoever has the necklace to know the truth about what happened."

Elizabeth looked over at Robin and Jessica. They both were staring at her as if she'd lost her mind.

"Don't look at me that way," she protested. "I know it doesn't make any sense. But how else do you explain what's going on?"

Jessica sighed. "Maybe you're right, Elizabeth. But all I can say is, if Lillian's trying to tell us something, she's going to have to try a little harder."

"No, I didn't say to rush," Becka said with a laugh. "I asked if you'd like to come with me to *rushes*."

It was early that afternoon, and the three girls had just arrived at the mansion.

"What are rushes?" Elizabeth asked.

"It's what we call the film we shot the day before. We have it developed right away, so we can see how it looks and make sure we like it."

"You mean the film of me?" Jessica asked nervously. She wasn't sure she wanted to see her big foul-up.

"I think there were a few other people in the shot too," Becka reminded her.

"Yeah, but they didn't blow it the way I did."

"It happens sometimes, Jasmine," Becka said. "Everybody blows lines."

"Not Shawn Brockaway," Jessica muttered.

"Well, Shawn's a very experienced, professional actor," Becka reassured her. "Of course, she's also a professional pain in the neck."

Becka led them down a hallway to a room that had once been a dining room. At one end was a projector, at the other end was a small screen, and in the middle were about two dozen chairs facing the screen. Becka pointed to some seats off to the side. "Sit there, gang. I have to go sit with my staff."

While the girls settled into their chairs, Becka joined Murray, Rolf, and several other members of her staff.

"She's awfully nice," Robin said, yawning.

"Yes, she is," Elizabeth agreed. "I'm going to be

able to write a great article about this. In fact, I'm taking so many notes, I may have to write a series of two or three articles. I think I'll call it 'The Making of a Movie'."

The lights went down and someone turned on the projector. Shawn appeared on the screen. They could hear Ashley Korman's voice, too, but only Shawn was visible.

"How come we can't see anyone but Shawn?" Jessica whispered to Elizabeth.

"Becka explained this. See, they take pictures of the same scene with several different cameras. I guess this is the film from just one of those cameras. Later on, they splice the different bits of film together. It's called editing."

"We're just blobs," Robin complained.

It was true. Shawn was in perfect focus, but the other girls were just fuzzy background figures.

The twins and Robin watched as the scene unfolded on the screen. They heard Lillian's and Hilda's now-familliar arguments once again. Then a third voice came from one of the fuzzy, out-of-focus figures behind Shawn. "Hey, you two!" she called. "This is supposed to be a party!"

Jessica winced and sank into her seat. "I sound so squeaky," she whispered.

"You do not," Elizabeth reassured her. "You sound great."

The camera pulled back a little, and the extras came into sharper focus. Jessica and Robin were finally visible, both of them looking concerned as they watched Lillian and Hilda fighting.

"Who's that?" Jessica whispered.

"Who's who?" Elizabeth whispered back.

"That girl. The one all the way at the back of the group."

Elizabeth leaned forward in her chair. The girl on the screen was staring straight at the camera. As a matter of fact, it almost seemed as if she were staring straight at the twins and Robin.

"That's not one of the extras," Robin said in a shaky whisper.

"I know," Jessica replied.

"Who is it, then?"

On screen the girl, still staring straight at the camera, separated herself from the group, and to Elizabeth's amazement, walked over and put her hand on Ashley Korman's shoulder.

The strange thing was, no one else seemed to notice. Not Ashley. Not Shawn. Not even Becka.

Elizabeth glanced over at Becka in disbelief. Why hadn't she noticed that some strange figure was wandering around in the middle of her movie?

"I have a bad feeling about this," Jessica muttered, her eyes riveted on the screen.

The pale, unsmiling girl let her hand rest on Hilda's shoulder for a moment. Then she walked over to the fireplace and pointed to a framed picture that rested on the mantel.

"I looked at that picture," Jessica whispered.

"It's supposed to be a picture of Lillian's mom in a wedding dress."

The girl on the screen kept her finger pointed at the picture for a moment. Then she pointed back to Hilda.

Suddenly the screen went white. Elizabeth, Jessica, and Robin all jumped at the sound of the film rattling as the reel ended.

"Not bad," Becka commented.

Someone snapped on the lights, and the three girls looked at each other in silence, their faces white.

"I don't think anyone else saw her," Robin whispered.

"I don't either." Jessica gulped. "I—I wonder who she is?"

"Or who she was," Elizabeth said in a low, shaky voice. "Remember what you said this morning, Jessica? *If Lillian's trying to tell us something, she's going to have to try a little harder.*" She took a deep breath. "Well, I think she just did."

"Can't we just drop it?" Robin said anxiously as she flopped onto Jessica's bed that evening.

"Don't you believe that was Lillian on the film?" Elizabeth demanded.

"Yes. No. I don't know—maybe," Robin said in frustration. "But even if it was, so what?"

"So she was trying to tell us something."

"Elizabeth," Robin said, "Lillian is dead. If that

was her, then it's some sort of a ghost. Do you really think we should be trying to help a ghost?"

"Robin may be right," Jessica said. "Who knows what Lillian wants?"

Elizabeth set her jaw in a look of determination that Jessica had seen many times before. "We have to try to figure this out," Elizabeth insisted.

"Look, Elizabeth, I'm scared," Robin said. "Really scared. Maybe this is a fun game to you, but personally, it gives me major creeps. First that stupid necklace makes me have a nightmare that I'm a dead girl, then the dead girl shows up in a movie, staring right at me. It's all too weird."

"She was trying to tell us something," Elizabeth insisted again, pacing back and forth across the room. "She put her hand on the girl playing Hilda. Then she pointed to Mrs. Keller's wedding picture, and back at Hilda again. What does it mean?"

"You're not listening," Robin said. "I don't *care* what it means."

"Maybe it means that Hilda was at Mrs. Keller's wedding," Jessica suggested.

Elizabeth shook her head. "Hilda was a little younger than Lillian. There's no way she could have been at the wedding."

"You know," Robin said, "in San Diego, we never have to deal with ghosts."

Jessica tossed a pillow at her cousin. "It's not like we're exactly Ghost Central here in Sweet Valley."

"Maybe it wasn't anything about weddings at all." Elizabeth looked thoughtful. "Maybe she was just trying to say something about a picture of Hilda, and that was the only picture she could find to point at."

"There were two other pictures on the mantel," Jessica said.

Elizabeth shrugged. "Maybe one of us should wear the necklace again and see if we can learn something new from the dreams."

"Not in a million years," Robin said firmly.

"I'm with Robin on that one," Jessica agreed. She didn't care *that* much about solving this mystery.

"You know what? Even *I* don't want to have one of those nightmares again," Elizabeth admitted.

Robin sighed. "Who knows, guys? Maybe Hilda got married."

Jessica shook her head. "Nice try, Robin, but Hilda's dead too."

"Nobody's really sure of that," Elizabeth said. "Becka just said they looked for her and couldn't find her anywhere."

"If they couldn't find her, then Hilda's either very lost, or very dead," Jessica said. She turned and noticed her sister staring at her strangely.

"Not if Robin's right, and Hilda did get married."

"What are you talking about, Elizabeth?"

"If Hilda got married, she probably would have

taken her husband's last name. Maybe Becka was looking for Hilda Tomlinson. But she could be Hilda Jones, or Hilda Smith, or anything."

"You know, Elizabeth," Jessica said slowly, "you could just be on to something. Becka told you that Hilda was released from that institution when she was eighteen, right? Suppose she did get married, and she's still alive somewhere?"

"Lillian's murderer, still alive," Elizabeth whispered. "And if we found her— "

"OK, that does it," Robin said, waving her hands. "I'm going home to San Diego. First it's nightmares, then it's ghosts, and now it's killers. I am not going to help you two with this."

"Don't you want to catch the person who killed Lillian?" Jessica asked.

"Excuse me, but catching killers is a job for the police, not for sixth-graders."

"You're right. But I don't see how we can convince the police about any of this," Elizabeth said with a sigh. "What would we tell them? We've had some bad dreams, so would you mind arresting this old lady?"

Jessica hesitated. Robin had a point. This could get very dangerous. And after all, what did they really have to go on?

She closed her eyes and let the memories flood back into her mind. She remembered the feeling of panic as she backed away toward the balcony, mute with terror, and the way her shoes slipped on the floor as the four-fingered hand snatched at her throat. She remembered falling, with lightning overhead and jagged rocks below.

Jessica opened her eyes. "I'm not letting her killer get away with this," she said firmly. "Lillian deserves that much."

Twelve

"Boy, people get married a lot," Elizabeth complained as she turned the spool of microfilm forward.

"Tell me about it," Robin said.

It was Wednesday morning, and Robin and the twins were at the Sweet Valley Public Library. Becka had given them the day off, since none of the scenes being shot that day required the extras.

Each of the girls was sitting at a microfilm machine with several spools of microfilmed newspapers piled beside her. They were searching for a wedding announcement for Hilda—an announcement that Elizabeth was secretly afraid might not even exist. Still, she reminded herself, they had to try, for Lillian's sake.

So far, the girls had looked through all the issues

of *The Sweet Valley Tribune* from 1945, 1946, and part of 1947. Hilda had been released from the institution on her eighteenth birthday, which had been in 1945. That had seemed as good a year to start searching as any.

"You know, she could have moved all the way across the country," Robin pointed out for the tenth time. "Then she wouldn't be in any of these newspapers at all. We could be totally wasting our time."

"I know," Elizabeth said patiently. "We'll just do a few more years and then we'll give up."

"Hey! Hey, you guys!" Jessica cried.

"What now?" Elizabeth asked in a tired voice. Jessica had already suggested three times that they should stop and go get something to eat.

"I've got her!"

Elizabeth leaped up and ran to look over Jessica's shoulder. The photograph on the viewer showed a young woman with a slightly sad smile. She was standing next to a man in a military uniform.

"Hilda Ellen Tomlinson exchanged vows with Lieutenant George Edgar Zalanski on August 26 at All Souls' Church," Jessica read aloud. "The groom's parents, Mrs. Della Margaret and Mr. Paul Darryl Zalanski, were both in attendance. The bride's parents, Mrs. Jane Kaella and Mr. Paxton Mead Tomlinson, are deceased."

"That must be her," Jessica said. "How many

people can there be named Hilda Tomlinson?"

"That's her," Elizabeth said confidently. "See? They say both her parents are deceased. Hilda— our Hilda—was an orphan. This must be her."

"All these names are confusing," Robin said, shaking her head.

"Zalanski. That's the name we're looking for. Hilda Tomlinson married George Zalanski. So she became Hilda Zalanski." Elizabeth grinned. "At least her name isn't Smith or something. I mean, how many *Zalanskis* can there be in the world?"

Elizabeth led the way over to the shelves where the telephone books were kept. She gave Robin and Jessica phone books from towns near Sweet Valley. Then she flipped open the Sweet Valley phone book to the Z's. It took less than ten seconds to find what she was looking for.

"H. Zalanski!" she announced.

"For all we know, it could be Herbert Zalanski," Jessica pointed out.

"Maybe, but I doubt it." Elizabeth pointed to the address by the name.

"101 Pearl Street," Jessica read. "That's down close to the beach."

"Right." Elizabeth said. "In fact, it's only a few minutes' walk from the Keller mansion."

"I don't get it," Robin said. "Why would Hilda want to live near the Keller mansion? Those couldn't be very happy memories for her."

Elizabeth smiled mysteriously. "If you two ever

read mystery novels, you'd understand. Lots of criminals do it. It's called returning to the scene of the crime."

Dear Mom and Dad:
This is probably dumb, but just in case, Jessica and I thought we'd better leave a note. I'm putting it here under the dinner plates because then you won't see it till dinner time. We should be home before then and I'll just tear up the note because you're not supposed to see it unless something goes wrong. Anyway, Jess and Robin and I are going to visit Hilda Zalanski, who used to be named Hilda Tomlinson. Her phone number and address are in the phone book. She's the one who was supposed to have killed Lillian Keller. I can't go into the whole story because it would take too long, plus you would think we were all nuts. Anyway, just in case we don't come back, you'll know where we went.
Love,
Elizabeth
P.S. Robin wants to add that she thinks Jessica and I are both crazy, but she doesn't want to chicken out.

Jessica read the note and handed it back to Elizabeth. "I guess that's OK," she said doubtfully.

"You don't really think there's any danger, do you?"

Elizabeth shook her head confidently. "Nope."

"I feel like one of those kids in a horror movie who's getting ready to do something really stupid, like open the door where the monster is hiding," Robin said. "And the whole audience is yelling *Don't go in there!*"

"I don't think Hilda is a monster," Elizabeth said.

"I wonder," Jessica said darkly.

Elizabeth slid the note under the dinner plates and the three girls headed out the door. It was a long walk to Hilda's house, and they had to pass the Keller mansion on the way.

"I guess Shawn's in there, making everyone's life impossible, as usual," Jessica remarked as they walked by. They found Hilda's house easily. It was a small cottage with a neat, attractive garden in the front yard. There were red rose bushes on both sides of the front gate. When Jessica glanced back, she was surprised to realize that she could just see a glimpse of the top floor of the Keller mansion.

They paused at the gate, staring at the front door of the cottage. "OK," Robin said nervously, "you guys go on ahead. I'll just wait right here."

"That's not a bad idea," Elizabeth said.

"It isn't?" Robin asked, looking hopeful.

"Just to be safe. It would be smart to leave one person out here."

"I thought you said you weren't worried," Jessica said.

"I'm not." Elizabeth shrugged. "But it never hurts to be careful."

"You know, usually *I'm* the one getting *you* involved in something dumb, Elizabeth," Jessica said, following her sister through the gate and down the front walk. "You're supposed to be the sensible twin."

Elizabeth didn't answer. Instead, she walked right up to the front door and pushed the doorbell.

"No one's home," Jessica said quickly. "Too bad, let's go."

Elizabeth grabbed her sister's arm and stopped her in midretreat. Then the door opened.

Jessica wasn't quite sure what she had expected to see, but it wasn't the kindly looking, gray-haired woman standing in front of them.

"Yes?" the woman said. "If you're selling Girl Scout cookies, I'm afraid I already bought two boxes."

"N-No ma'am, that's not it," Elizabeth said.

"Then how may I help you?"

"It's kind of a long story," Elizabeth began. "You see . . . uh . . . we—"

"Are you Hilda Tomlinson?" Jessica blurted.

The old woman's eyes narrowed, and her mouth tightened into a grim line. "I don't see that that's any of your business. Who sent you here?"

Elizabeth and Jessica exchanged a glance.

"I asked who sent you here?" the old woman repeated more sharply.

"Lillian Keller," Elizabeth said in a near whisper. "Lillian sent us."

The old woman's eyes grew cold at the mention of Lillian's name. "Lillian Keller has been dead for decades," she said at last.

"We know," Jessica said softly.

Hilda scowled. "Then how could she have sent you?"

"I know this is going to sound ridiculous," Elizabeth said, "but she's been in our dreams."

"Get out of here. I don't know what you two think you're up to, but get off my property."

The twins looked at each other and reluctantly began to walk away. They'd gone only a few steps when Elizabeth stopped and turned to face Hilda squarely.

"Mrs. Zalanski?" she said. "The necklace *did* belong to your mother. You were right."

Hilda looked startled. She stared at Elizabeth wordlessly.

"Behind the red stone," Elizabeth went on, "there are engraved initials. *J.K.T.* Your mother's name was Jane Kaella Tomlinson—J.K.T."

Hilda staggered back as though she'd been struck. "Yes," she said in a hoarse whisper. "My mother's initials. It *was* her necklace. But . . ." For a moment, her voice trailed off. Her eyes became bright with tears. "I was so young. I didn't understand.

When my mother died, the necklace was passed to her sister, Lillian's mother. My aunt never realized how much that necklace meant to me. She didn't know that when I saw it again, it would bring back every terrible memory of my mother's death." She shook her head as if to clear her mind. "Please come in, girls. Please."

Inside, the cottage was neat, but dark and a little dusty. The furnishings were plain and threadbare. It was obvious that Hilda didn't have much money. She motioned for them to sit on the couch. "Just a moment. I'll get us some tea."

She reappeared a few minutes later with a teapot and cups on a tray. She seemed to have regained control of her emotions. Elizabeth and Jessica each accepted one of the steaming cups of tea, and sipped slowly while Hilda spoke.

"Of course, it was all right for Lillian to have that necklace. I was just overcome with anger. You see, it seemed to me that Lillian had everything. Most of all, she had parents who loved her, and I missed my parents terribly. When I saw her so happy with the necklace, a necklace that would have been mine if my own mother had lived—well, I just snapped. I was furious. Just furious."

Jessica remembered the Hilda of her nightmares—a little girl, red-faced with anger. It was hard to believe that angry little girl had grown to become this sad old woman.

"Anyway, we fought. But then, we fought often.

It was both our faults, really—mine for being jealous, and hers for being resentful that I had come to live with her family." Hilda shrugged. "Still, beneath it all, we were friends, Lillian and I. Almost like sisters, really."

When she fell silent, Elizabeth spoke up. "We know some of the story, Mrs. Zalanski. They're making a movie about it over at the Keller mansion, and we were hired as extras. Actually, Jessica—" she motioned to her sister, "is doing most of the acting. I'm writing an article for my class paper."

"I'm Luella," Jessica said.

Hilda laughed. "I hope not, dear. Luella was a stupid, spoiled child." Then she turned serious again. "I read about the movie in the newspaper. I was afraid that somehow they might track me down and stir up all my old memories." She sighed heavily.

"We're sorry if that's what we've done," Jessica said. She knew Hilda was supposed to be a murderer, but somehow, sitting there having tea with her, it was hard not to feel sorry for her.

Hilda poured herself a second cup of tea. "I suppose they have me as the one who pushed Lillian off the balcony?"

"That's what it says in the script," Elizabeth admitted.

"That's what everyone believes," Hilda said.

"Did you do it?" Elizabeth asked softly. She couldn't help it.

Hilda's eyes narrowed again, and Jessica could see an echo of the temper she'd had as a child. "No. No, I did not do it. I did not!"

"Then who did?" Elizabeth asked.

Hilda sagged into her chair, the anger past. "I don't know. Only two people ever did know the answer to that question. One, of course, was Lillian herself. The other—"

"Was the real murderer," Jessica whispered.

Thirteen

"I fought with Lillian over the necklace," Hilda continued in a soft, faraway voice, "and she ran upstairs. For a moment I just stayed at the party." She gave a sad smile. "Which by then, as you can imagine, wasn't much of a party anymore. But then I began to feel terrible. I knew it wasn't Lillian's fault that her mother had given her a present I thought should belong to me. It was her birthday, and I had ruined it. So I headed upstairs to make up with her."

"Wasn't Lillian's mother there?" Jessica interrupted. "It seems like she should have straightened things out between you two."

"I wish my aunt had been there," Hilda said wistfully. "But she was in the parlor, with the parents of the other children." She looked at the twins. "How old are you two?"

"Twelve," Elizabeth answered.

"I thought as much," Hilda said. "Well, then you can understand. This was supposed to be our first real party without parents. Of course, they were right around the corner, but we thought we were very grand and adult." She took a sip of her tea. "Anyway, when I got upstairs, I saw that the door to my aunt's room was open, and I thought I heard noises in there. So in I went, and once inside I heard a cry—faint, but distinct—coming from the balcony. I ran out onto the balcony, but not a soul was there. I thought I was hearing things, until the cry came again, and I looked over the edge . . ."

Jessica clutched her teacup so tightly she thought it might crack. She glanced over at Elizabeth, who was sitting rigidly in her seat, biting her lower lip nervously.

Hilda cleared her throat. "I saw Lillian hanging by her fingers from a little ledge just below the balcony. Somehow she'd managed to grab hold of it. Her legs were swinging wildly, but there was nothing for them to reach. It was a straight drop down, and I could see that her fingers were losing their grip. I screamed for help, but no one seemed to hear, so I leaned out over the railing and reached for her hand. I tried to grab her wrist, but I was in danger of falling over too."

Hilda paused for a moment and closed her eyes, as though the memory was too much to bear. When she opened her eyes, she reached for her teacup with trembling fingers. It clattered against the saucer, the only sound in the silent room.

"Lillian tried to say something," Hilda continued at last. "I'll never forget it—*H-H-H*—as if she was trying to scream for help, or perhaps to say my name. But she couldn't speak. I saw her hands slip and made a desperate lunge. I caught the sleeve of her dress in my hand . . ."

The old woman covered her eyes with her hands and was silent for several minutes "I couldn't save her," she whispered. "The sleeve tore, and she fell."

Elizabeth and Jessica exchanged a glance. There'd been nothing in their dreams about Hilda reaching to save Lillian.

"Just then, Harry ran in and began shouting for help. Everyone saw the sleeve in my hand, and they knew Lillian and I had fought. They drew their own conclusions."

"Who was Harry?" Jessica asked.

"Harry Dennison," Hilda said. "He was the family chauffeur. A young man, barely eighteen at the time." The memory made her smile a little. "He always told us girls that some day he would be rich like we were. We thought he was very handsome, and of course, he was terribly vain."

"Vain?" Elizabeth repeated.

Hilda laughed. "Oh, yes, he was vain, all right. You could tell by the way he dressed, and always made sure his hair was neatly combed. And of course, he always walked around with his hand in his pocket."

"Do you know what happened to him?" Elizabeth asked.

"No. I lost track of him and everyone else when I was sent away." Again Hilda's eyes grew troubled. "Of course, it was Harry who really cinched the case against me."

"But you say you didn't push Lillian," Jessica pressed. "How could Harry have cinched the case?"

"Harry told the Kellers that he'd been passing by in the hallway outside the bedroom, and he'd happened to see something out of the corner of his eye that looked odd. He said he stopped, turned to look more closely, and saw me pushing Lillian over the railing."

"He said he *saw* you do it?" Elizabeth asked.

"That's what he told the Kellers. Of course, it really wasn't Harry's fault. I suppose he must have seen me lunging forward, trying to reach over the railing and pull Lillian back up. But you know memories can be funny. Harry swore he saw Lillian and me standing on the balcony, and me pushing her. But all he could really have seen was me."

"Were you ever arrested?" Elizabeth asked.

"No. The Kellers told the police they thought I was mad. Crazy. They were good people, and they didn't want to punish me as much as they wanted to help me. So the police didn't pursue the case, and the Kellers sent me to a psychiatric institution—a mental hospital for young people who are criminally insane." There was no missing the bitterness in Hilda's voice. "But I wasn't mad. I was innocent. I *am* innocent. Since I left the institution though, I've kept silent. I married and lived all over the world with my husband, but when he died, I felt drawn back here. Don't ask me why." Hilda smiled sadly. "Maybe I am crazy, after all, coming back to the place where I lost any hope for happiness "

The three of them sat in silence.

At last Elizabeth took a deep breath. "Mrs. Zalanski, why did Harry keep his hand in his pocket?"

Hilda sighed. "I suppose he was hiding it."

"But why?" Jessica blurted.

"He'd had some kind of accident and cut himself. He was very self-conscious about it. You see, he'd lost one of the fingers on his left hand."

"It's about time!" Robin exploded as the twins rejoined her on the street outside. "I was about ready to call the police."

"It's OK, Robin," Elizabeth said. "I don't think we need to be afraid of Hilda."

As they walked along the beach, the twins told their cousin what Hilda had told them.

"Do you believe her?" Robin asked when they had finished.

Jessica nodded. "She seemed way too nice to be a murderer."

"Only one thing bothers me," Elizabeth said with a frown. "There wasn't anything in my dreams about Hilda trying to pull Lillian to safety."

"I told you that I saw Hilda's face leaning over me," Robin said. "I mean, leaning over *Lillian*. Hilda's face was the last thing she saw."

"But maybe that was because Hilda really was the one who pushed her over the balcony," Elizabeth countered. "I wish we'd gotten more details in the dreams."

"Did Hilda ask why you were questioning her?" Robin asked.

"Yes, and we told her," Elizabeth answered.

Robin gasped. "You mean you told her about the necklace and the nightmares and the image on the film?"

"Everything," Elizabeth confirmed.

"She must have thought you were nuts."

"Actually, she didn't have much to say after that. I think she believed us, though," Elizabeth said. "She just nodded and whispered 'Thanks, Lil'."

"'Thanks, Lil'?" Robin repeated doubtfully. "You mean like she was thanking Lillian? That sure doesn't sound like someone who killed Lillian."

"It sure doesn't," Elizabeth said.

"So if Hilda didn't do it, who did?" Robin asked.

The twins looked at each other for a moment.

"The man with four fingers," they said together.

"Right. And who is that?"

"Harry, the chauffeur," Jessica answered.

"The chauffeur?" Robin said with a grin. "Steven said it was always the butler who did it."

"I'm almost sure it was Harry," Jessica said firmly. "Now all we have to do is find him."

As they passed the Keller mansion, Elizabeth paused to gaze at it pensively. "I don't think we'll have to go very far," she said.

The next day, the girls were at the mansion bright and early. "Hey, what's that thing over there?" Jessica asked as they crossed the grounds. She pointed to a group of workmen who were inflating what looked like a gigantic air mattress.

"You two go on in," Elizabeth said. "I'll find out." She pulled out her pad and pencil. She had been so busy lately trying to solve the mystery of Lillian's death that she'd nearly forgotten about her *Sixers* article.

"Hi," she said to a man in shorts and a tank top who was busy overseeing the effort.

"Hey, kid, don't get any closer, all right?" the man said.

"OK. But what are you doing? What's the bag for?"

"Who are you?" the man asked a little suspiciously.

"My name's Elizabeth Wakefield. I'm writing a story for my class newspaper."

"The director know you're here?"

"Becka and I are old friends," Elizabeth said, exaggerating just a little. "I've been interviewing her, mostly. But this looks interesting."

The man grinned. "It is. My name's Will Shipley. I'm the stunt coordinator." He looked over at Elizabeth's pad as she wrote his name down. "S-H-I-P-L-E-Y."

"What's a stunt coordinator?"

"I'm the guy who organizes all the stunts in a movie. When you see a car crash, or someone flying through a window, that's a stunt person at work. This time we're going to be doing a fall." He gestured toward the big air bag. "We're checking the equipment today so we can be sure it's in good shape when it's needed."

"I didn't think there were going to be any stunts in this movie."

"There aren't many. Just one, really. The one where the kid goes over the side. You know, Shawn Brockaway."

"You mean when she gets pushed off the balcony?"

"Yeah, that's it. Well, what we do is have this big bag beneath the balcony, set up over the rocks. She falls, lands on the bag, no problem."

"Is it safe?" Elizabeth asked, eyeing the bag doubtfully.

"Oh, sure. The only problem is that setting it up on the rocks is tricky. It's kind of a narrow area, and when the tide comes in, the waves splash like crazy. Still, it's got to be an improvement, right?"

"An improvement?" Elizabeth echoed.

Will grinned. "An improvement over landing like the real little girl did, right on those rocks."

When Elizabeth got inside, she found Jessica and Robin already in their costumes and makeup. They were in the ballroom preparing to film another party scene. Maria, Mandy, and the rest of the extras were there too. But Shawn was nowhere to be seen.

Jessica and Robin detached themselves from the group to join Elizabeth. "This is so confusing," Jessica complained. "I don't know why they can't just shoot the movie in the right order. Becka told us that today we're doing a scene that happened *before* the fight scene we did the other day. Does that make any sense?"

"I guess it does to a movie director," Elizabeth said. "In the end, she'll put it all in the right order."

"I know," Jessica said, "but how can we perform without knowing what's going on *emotionally* in the scene?"

Elizabeth suppressed a grin. "Well, what are you supposed to be doing today?"

"We have to mill around behind Lillian as she talks to her mother," Robin explained.

"Mill around?" Elizabeth echoed.

"Yes, mill around," Jessica said defensively.

"Becka said milling around is very important. It has to look like real milling, not like a bunch of people pretending to mill."

"While I'm milling, I have to pick up a tiny sandwich off that table—" Robin pointed to a table loaded with food, "and turn to face Jessica and pretend to eat it."

"Why not just eat it?"

"I thought of that," Robin said. "But it's not a real sandwich. It's made of wax. Becka said real food attracts flies, and they don't want flies all over the place."

"I have to watch Robin pretend to eat the sandwich," Jessica said. "Then on my cue, I have to take her hand and lead her across the room as if we're going to talk to someone. It's a very important part," she finished proudly.

"Not as important as eating a sandwich," Robin countered.

"You don't even really get to eat it," Jessica argued.

Elizabeth rolled her eyes. "Where is Becka, anyway?" she asked.

"I think she's in Shawn's dressing room," Jessica said meaningfuly. "I heard one of the crew saying that Shawn's throwing a tantrum."

"What else is new?"

"So as usual, we're all hanging out again, waiting for little Ms. Brockaway to emerge," Robin said, sighing.

"Luckily, after this we have only two more scenes to do with her," Jessica said. "Tomorrow there's just some more milling, I guess, then the next day there's the big party scene. Becka calls it the cake scene. It's where they wheel in this monstrous five-foot-tall birthday cake for Lillian. It's going to be the final scene for the extras." Jessica smiled a little wistfully.

"The bad news is we won't be working here anymore," Robin said. "The good news is we won't ever have to get near Shawn Brockaway again."

"Here comes the brat now," Jessica muttered, looking across the set.

Elizabeth watched Robin and Jessica dash back to their places. *Only two more days of shooting for the extras*, she thought anxiously. That didn't leave her much time to solve the mystery.

Later that afternoon, Elizabeth found Mr. Brooks adjusting a light stand with one hand. As usual, his left hand was hidden in his pocket.

Sooner or later you'll have to take that hand out of your pocket, Elizabeth thought. But as she watched him work, she realized just how good the old man was at doing everything with one hand.

That matched what Hilda had told them—that Harry Dennison, the chauffeur, was vain, and didn't like people to see his injured hand. Mr. Brooks was about the right age. He had to be almost seventy, although there was no way for Elizabeth to know for sure.

Let me see it, Harry, Elizabeth thought, trying to will him to reveal his hand. Casually she moved a little closer. But as she walked, one of the many cables lying on the floor seemed to writhe like a snake. It wrapped itself around Elizabeth's foot and she tripped, falling forward. Desperately she grabbed at something to stop her fall. Her hand caught a pole that supported one of the big stage lights, and the light came crashing down.

But Mr. Brooks moved swiftly. He caught the pole just before the light smashed into the floor.

Elizabeth sprawled on the ground amid the cables. She looked over and saw Mr. Brooks, struggling with *both* hands to raise the light back up.

"Four-finger Harry," Elizabeth whispered. "I've found you."

Fourteen

"*Shh,*" Jessica whispered.

"*Shh* yourself," Robin snapped.

"Both of you *shh,*" Elizabeth said.

The three girls were sneaking up the stairs that led to Mrs. Keller's bedroom. After the day's shooting, they had slipped into an unused dressing room and waited until everyone else had gone home. Jessica had called Mrs. Wakefield to tell her that they would be a little late.

"Why are we being quiet?" Robin asked.

"Because we're not supposed to be here," Elizabeth replied.

"But everyone went home," Jessica said.

"Besides, all this sneaking and whispering just makes this seem scarier," Robin added.

Elizabeth thought for a moment. Robin had a

point. "OK, no more whispering. But don't make *too* much noise, all right? I know everyone went home, but you never know. Someone might wander past on the grounds and notice something."

"This is really giving me the willies," Jessica murmured as they continued up the stairs. "I've never been up here, but I feel as if I've seen it all before. I know exactly what we're going to see when we get to the top of the stairs."

Elizabeth nodded sympathetically. "That's how I felt when I came up here before."

Robin paused for a moment, gripping the railing so tightly that her knuckles were white. "Are you *sure* we really have to do this?"

"Sure I'm sure," Elizabeth said, trying to sound confident. "Detectives in mystery stories do it all the time. It's called reenacting the crime."

"Only we're reenacting nightmares," Jessica pointed out. "I'll bet you haven't read *that* in one of your mystery novels."

Elizabeth fell silent. It was true. This was different—and a lot spookier.

They reached the top landing and paused. The sun was just beginning to set outside, and black shadows had turned the hallway into a gloomy tunnel.

"I guess I don't have to tell you where the bedroom is, do I?" Elizabeth tried to joke.

Jessica and Robin giggled nervously. "I guess not," Robin said.

They made their way timidly down the hall. The door to the bedroom was shut. Elizabeth reached for the knob and turned it, holding her breath as she slowly swung the door open. "Please, tell me there's a light in there," she said, staring into the dark room.

Robin looked thoughtful. "Wait a sec. I think I remember a light switch on the left, just inside the door."

"And you want *me* to find it?"

"You're closest," Robin pointed out.

Elizabeth took a deep breath and extended her arm into the dark room. She slid her hand up and down the wall, then felt something. A second later the room was lit with a yellowish glow. "Wow, you have detailed dreams."

"I'm glad," Jessica said. "I'd much rather do this in the light."

As soon as Elizabeth stepped inside the room, a flood of images from her nightmares washed over her. She also remembered the day Harold Brooks— or Harry Dennison—had discovered her up here.

I might have been standing here face-to-face with a murderer, she thought. It wasn't a very comforting thought.

"There's the balcony," Jessica said, pointing to a pair of French doors draped with heavy curtains. "Behind those doors."

"Better open it," Elizabeth advised. "They were open the day that . . . you know."

"Don't look at me," Jessica said.

"There's nothing to be afraid of," Elizabeth said firmly, although she wasn't sure she believed her own words. She squared her shoulders, walked over to the balcony doors, and threw them open.

A moist evening breeze blew in. The last few rays of sunlight spilled over the balcony. Elizabeth shuddered. This was the very spot where Lillian had fallen to her death. *Been* pushed *to her death*, she corrected herself.

"Let's go out there," she said.

"Why?" Robin asked suspiciously.

"We're supposed to be recalling all the clues from our dreams to see if Hilda's story could possibly be true," Elizabeth reminded her cousin. "So come on out and quit being such a chicken."

The three girls stepped gingerly out onto the narrow balcony. By cautiously leaning over the railing, they could see the sharp black rocks below. The tide was just coming in, and foaming waves were breaking over the rocks, sending spray into the air.

"The tide was higher on the night she died," Robin commented in a low voice.

Jessica nodded. "It was darker out too. It was daytime, but the storm was so bad that it seemed like night."

"And there was lightning," Elizabeth added. She pointed downward. "See? That could be the little ledge that Hilda claimed Lillian was holding on to."

"It's too narrow for her to hang on for long," Robin pointed out.

Jessica sighed. "She *didn't* hang on for long, did she?"

"Hold on to me," Elizabeth said suddenly. She started to lean over the railing of the balcony.

"Elizabeth!" Jessica cried in alarm. "Are you nuts?"

"I want to see if Hilda could possibly have reached Lillian. But I also want you two to hang on tight to my waist," she warned. "I've already felt what it was like to fall onto those rocks in my dreams. I don't want to do it for real."

Robin and Jessica grabbed Elizabeth around the waist and held on tight as she leaned as far as she could over the side. Her head swam as she gazed at the jagged rocks below. She stretched out her hand, straining as far as she could, and managed to touch the narrow ledge where Lillian might have desperately clung to life.

"OK, pull me up," she said urgently, as her heart quickened in panic.

"Well?" Jessica demanded when Elizabeth was standing straight again.

Elizabeth nodded. "She could have done it. Hilda could have reached just far enough to touch Lillian's fingers or grab the sleeve of her dress."

"Then Hilda's telling the truth," Robin said. "Now let's go home."

"Not yet. We still don't know the whole truth,"

Elizabeth said. "I want to try acting out the story."

"This is *not* my idea of acting," Robin grumbled.

"Jessica, you be Lillian," Elizabeth directed.

"Somehow I just knew you were going to say that," Jessica said. She sighed. "Oh well, I guess it *is* the starring role."

"Great. Now go out into the hallway and come back into the bedroom just the way it was in your dream. Robin and I will watch and see if we remember anything different."

Jessica stepped out into the hallway and immediately returned with a dramatic sweep of her hand. "It is I, Lillian," she announced.

"Cut the dramatic stuff," Elizabeth advised.

Jessica frowned. "OK, OK," she said with a shrug. "So she walked in, right?" She took half a dozen quick steps forward. "And she stopped right about here."

"Why did she stop?" Elizabeth asked.

"Because she heard a noise," Robin offered. "A rustling noise from—" Robin scanned the room, "from over there." She pointed to the dressing table near the bed.

"There was a jewelry box on the dressing table," Jessica added.

Elizabeth nodded. "And the box was open."

"Of course it was open," Jessica said. "The man with four fingers had his hand in it."

"Why?" Elizabeth asked.

"Why what?" Jessica said.

"Why would Harry, the chauffeur, be up here digging around in Mrs. Keller's jewelry box?"

"There's only one reason I can think of," Robin said. "He was stealing the jewels."

"But there was nothing in the newspaper, or in the movie script, about stolen jewels. That's the kind of thing somebody would have noticed," Elizabeth pointed out.

"Maybe Lillian walked in just as he was getting ready to steal them," Jessica suggested.

"It would have been the perfect time for him to do it," Elizabeth said. "According to the script, all the kids were downstairs at the party. The adults were in the living room, and most of the servants were either waiting on the kids or the adults."

"OK, so Lillian walked in and saw him stealing," Jessica continued. "He knew she would tell, so—"

"So he killed her," Elizabeth said softly.

"But first, he decided to snatch the necklace from around her neck," Robin said. "I remember that very clearly from my dream."

"I know just what he was thinking," Elizabeth said, nodding. "Lillian would fall to the rocks, and everyone would assume that the necklace had washed away in the surf. Harry could keep the necklace and no one would ever know."

"Why didn't he take the jewels in the jewelry box, too?" Robin asked.

"How could he?" Jessica said. "With Lillian dead, everyone would have figured out right away that her death had something to do with the stolen jewels. He really couldn't take them."

"He *could* safely take the necklace, but then he dropped it," Elizabeth concluded. "So he got nothing. In the end, Harry killed Lillian for nothing." She fell silent for a moment, remembering the terrifying feeling she'd had in her dream as she'd plummeted toward the rocks.

"And then Hilda came in," Jessica said, breaking the silence.

Elizabeth sat down on the edge of the dusty bed. "Harry must have left Lillian hanging on the ledge and run to hide when he heard Hilda coming." She glanced around the room. "In the closet, I'll bet. He saw her struggling to rescue Lillian. But when he heard Lillian's scream, and saw poor Hilda holding nothing but Lillian's sleeve, he realized she was the perfect person to blame the murder on."

Jessica nodded. "It could be. It certainly all fits with our memories."

"It has to be right," Robin said.

"No, it doesn't." Elizabeth shook her head. "Not necessarily."

"Come on, Elizabeth," Jessica moaned. "Don't you want to get out of this creepy place?"

Elizabeth held up one finger. "Just let me try one more thing. It could be that we're confused about what we saw in our nightmares, and Harry's story really was the truth." She turned to

Robin. "It's your turn to act. You play Harry."

Robin sighed. "How come Jessica gets the good role?"

"Good role?" Jessica echoed. "I get murdered, Robin!"

"Good point. OK, what do I do, Elizabeth?"

"Harry claimed he was in the hall when he saw Hilda push Lillian. Go out into the hallway. I'm going onto the balcony to pretend to be Hilda, pushing Lillian over the side."

Robin stepped out into the hall and Elizabeth pushed Jessica toward the balcony railing. "Watch it, Lizzie," Jessica warned. "Don't push too hard!"

"How does it look?" Elizabeth called out.

"I can't see you guys," Robin said. She walked back into the bedroom, shaking her head. "I couldn't see a thing. Harry would have had to be able to see around corners in order to see Hilda push Lillian."

Elizabeth took a deep breath. "I thought so. Well, that proves what we suspected. Harry is a—"

"Freeze! Nobody move an inch!"

Fifteen

◇

"For Pete's sake, Tony, can't you see they're just three girls?" Becka cried. She laughed. "Tony's our security guard. He called and told me there was a light on up here."

Jessica paused to make certain her heart was still beating. Tony had scared her half to death.

Becka gazed at them doubtfully. "Now, how about if you three tell me what you're doing up here where you are definitely not supposed to be?"

"You would never believe it," Jessica said wearily.

"Try me."

"No, really—"

"Really."

Elizabeth cleared her throat nervously. "Could this be private, just between us?"

Becka hesitated for a moment, then waved the security guard away. "I don't think I'm in too much danger from these hardened criminals," she told him. She sat down on the bed. "Let's hear it," she said when Tony had gone. "And it had better be good."

Elizabeth took a deep breath and launched into the story, beginning with the discovery of the necklace in the surf. She told Becka about their weird attraction to the necklace, and about their terrifying nightmares. She even told her about the strange image they'd seen on the rushes. And, of course, she told her everything they had learned about Lillian, Hilda, and Harry.

When Elizabeth had finished, Becka nodded slowly, a small smile on her face. "You realize that's a completely crazy story, don't you?" she said at last.

"I'm not surprised you don't believe us," Jessica said, shrugging hopelessly.

"I didn't say I don't believe it," Becka said sharply. "Don't forget I'm the woman who gave the world *Grandpa's Ghost*. I'm not saying I'm a big believer in ghosts, but I do like to keep an open mind. And even if I were inclined to think this story's a little farfetched, there's something else I know—" she paused, staring out toward the balcony thoughtfully. "Something about Harold Brooks that you don't. See, Harold was a lighting technician in movies for thirty years. Then he retired. In fact, he retired ten years ago. But when I started getting ready to do this movie, he showed up on the set and told me he *had* to work on this movie. He even volunteered to work for free." Becka stroked her chin thoughtfully. "I figured I could use a guy *that* enthusiastic."

"Why would he want to come back here, though?" Robin asked. "You'd think it would be the last place on earth he'd ever want to be."

"I think I may have an answer for that," Becka said. "Early on, when we were first checking out this location, a copy of the script disappeared. We looked everywhere and eventually found Harold reading it. Not just reading it like a curious person might do, but devouring it, as if it was the most important thing he'd ever read."

"He was afraid something might come out during the making of the movie that would unmask him," Elizabeth said.

"If what you say is true," Becka replied, "then that's exactly what happened."

"I've arranged for us to be alone for this screening," Becka said the next morning. "These are the rushes from the day before yesterday. I want you three to watch them with me and tell me if your ghostly friend shows up." She pounded the side of her head with her palm. "Will you listen to me? And I pretend to be so reasonable."

"You and me both," Elizabeth said with a laugh, sitting down next to Becka.

"We probably should have brought the necklace in," Jessica said.

"We think that's what Lillian uses to communicate with us—through the dreams, and maybe somehow with the film, too," Elizabeth explained.

Becka held up her hands. "I don't want anything to do with that necklace." She lowered her voice. "Personally, I really don't want to see a ghost, either."

"But you believe it's *possible* that Lillian's a ghost, right?" Jessica asked.

"Like I said, I'm keeping an open mind," Becka replied. "That still doesn't mean I want to *see* her. After all, as soon as we're done here, I have to go back to the set and deal with Shawn. That's enough horror for anyone."

The girls laughed. "Snap off the lights, someone," Becka instructed. "I'll start the projector."

The screen flashed to life. It was what Jessica called the milling scene. While the extras wandered around, Shawn talked to the woman who was playing Mrs. Keller.

"I don't see anything," Elizabeth said after a moment.

"What are you talking about?" Jessica demanded. "I see *me*—and I'm milling very well, in my opinion."

"An award-winning mill, if I ever saw one," Becka agreed.

Suddenly Robin gasped. "There she is!"

"Where?" Jessica asked, straining to catch a glimpse of Lillian.

"What do you see?" Becka asked anxiously.

"She's behind the table!" Robin said. "Can't you guys see her?"

"Now I do," Elizabeth said as she squinted at the screen. "But she's almost invisible. I can practically see right through her."

"No, she's not invisible," Robin said. "I can see her just fine. Not as well as the other day, but well enough."

"I don't see anything," Jessica exclaimed, feeling frustrated. "Except for my milling."

"Me neither," Becka said.

The film flickered to a halt, and Jessica got up to snap on the lights. "Are you guys playing a trick on me? I didn't see Lillian on that film at all, and the other day she was perfectly clear."

"I saw her almost as clearly as the first time," Robin said.

"Hmmm." Elizabeth twisted a strand of hair around her finger thoughtfully. "Robin, you were the person to wear the necklace most recently. Then me, then Jessica. Maybe the power of the necklace fades the longer you're away from it."

"That would make sense," Becka agreed. Then she covered her face and groaned. "What am I saying? *Nothing* about this makes any sense at all."

"I think Elizabeth's right," Jessica said after a moment of thought. "As soon as I let Elizabeth have the necklace, the nightmares stopped and my attraction to it wore off. And now look—I've totally lost the ability to see Lillian on the film." She couldn't help smiling. It was a relief not to have to worry about ghosts popping up in the middle of movies.

"Robin," Becka said, "you say you could still see her. What was she doing?"

Robin nodded. "The message was really clear this time. All she did was hold up her left hand, like this." Robin demonstrated. "Then she folded down one finger, so it looked as if she had only four. Then she looked right at me and nodded her head."

"We've got our man," Becka said.

"Now we have to think of a way to catch him," Elizabeth added.

"I could absolutely kill that girl," Mandy exploded that afternoon when filming had finally finished for the day.

All afternoon, Shawn had been on her absolute worst behavior. When Mandy had bumped against her chair, Shawn had called her a klutz. When Maria had blown a line, Shawn had sneered, "That's why you're washed up, Maria." When Robin had sneezed during a take, Shawn had thrown a plastic sandwich at her, barely missing her head.

And when Jessica had done nothing except

stand right where she was told to, Shawn had still insisted on calling her "the airhead who likes ice cream."

"I can't stand her as much as you can't stand her," Jessica said fervently.

"I can't stand her even worse," Maria chimed in.

"No, I'm the one who *really* can't stand her," Robin said.

"Where's Elizabeth?" Mandy asked Jessica. "She should be here to not stand Shawn too. After all, Shawn yelled at Elizabeth for staring at her."

Jessica grinned. "Yeah, and I loved how she answered in her usual calm Elizabeth voice, 'I'm sorry for staring, but I think you have a booger hanging out of your nose.'"

Mandy laughed. "So, where is she?"

Jessica looked away evasively. "She had some things to do."

"Do you two want to walk home with us?" Maria asked.

"No, we're supposed to meet Elizabeth here in a little while," Robin said.

"But everyone's leaving," Mandy pointed out.

"Don't worry, she'll be here." Jessica said. "You know Elizabeth."

As Jessica and Robin said good-bye to the others, Jessica noticed Becka heading for the door. She watched Becka pause as she passed Harry, as if suddenly remembering something.

"Harry," Becka called.

"Was there something you needed?" he asked.

"I hate to ask this of you, but we really need to have those lights in the ballroom adjusted. We're getting a lot of glare, and I want them to be ready to go first thing in the morning."

"But that could take a long time," he complained.

"Sorry," Becka said with a shrug, sauntering off.

Jessica looked over at Robin. "Time to go to wardrobe," she whispered.

The two girls slipped away to the wardrobe room. They met Elizabeth inside. "Everything going OK?" Elizabeth asked.

"So far, so good," Jessica said, trying to sound casual.

"Becka asked him to stay, and he's still here," Robin added.

Elizabeth nodded thoughtfully. "Well, everything is set. At least I hope it is."

"What do you mean, you *hope* it is?" Jessica demanded.

"It's nothing," Elizabeth assured her sister. "But—well, maybe I should be the one doing the main role."

"Give me a break. This is the acting job of a lifetime. This is *my* role."

Elizabeth smiled. "You're right. You're the actress."

"And you're the planner." Jessica grinned and gave her sister a hug. "I know it will all work out fine."

"Remember," Elizabeth said, "if you get scared, just yell *Unicorns*. That'll be the signal. OK?"

"Unicorns. I couldn't forget that, could I?" Jessica asked nervously.

Elizabeth glanced at her watch. "Let's get you changed. It's almost time."

Jessica quickly removed her own costume and put on Shawn's—an old-fashioned one very similar to the one Lillian had been wearing the day she died.

Then Robin and Elizabeth began applying makeup. Not just on Jessica's face, but on her neck, arms, and legs as well.

"That looks awful," Jessica commented as she caught sight of herself in the mirror.

"It's supposed to," Elizabeth pointed out.

"The sacrifices we actresses have to make for our art!" Jessica stood up and twirled around. "So how do I look?"

"Pretty bad," Robin said.

"There's just one thing left," Elizabeth said quietly.

Instantly Jessica's grin disappeared. "I know."

Elizabeth went over to her backpack, which was sitting on a chair nearby. She reached inside and pulled out a wad of white tissue paper. Handling it gingerly, she slowly unwrapped the package.

Jessica watched as the gems began to appear—the smaller diamonds first, then the huge red ruby. They were all clean and sparkling.

"It took me a while to get the rest cleaned up," Elizabeth remarked. "I figure I just won't go to sleep tonight, if you know what I mean."

"I'm planning on staying up all night myself," Jessica agreed.

"Hey, if you two can't sleep, I can't either," Robin said. She picked up the necklace. Then she stepped over and draped it around her cousin's neck.

Sixteen

Jessica crept slowly and silently onto the set. Harry was working only a few feet away with his back to her, whistling softly to himself.

The ballroom was empty except for the two of them. Jessica jumped as she heard a deep rumbling sound. *It's only thunder,* she realized, trying to calm herself down.

She took a deep breath. *It's time, Jess,* she told herself. *You wanted to be an actress. Now here's your chance.*

"I'm taking this straight upstairs and putting it in Mother's jewelry box where *you* can't get at it!" Jessica cried out suddenly.

Harry gasped and spun around as Jessica made a dash toward the stairs.

Jessica felt a moment of triumph. She'd been

hoping to shock Harry, and she obviously had. And who could blame him? She was wearing a dress like Lillian's, and was covered from head to toe in bluish makeup. She looked very much like Lillian . . . a very dead Lillian.

But as she ran past Harry, she saw his eyes focus. Not on the dress or the makeup, but on the necklace. She was sure of it. It was as if all he had really seen were the jewels around her neck.

As she took the stairs, Jessica felt the cold metal against her throat—just as Lillian had. She reached the hallway and dashed toward Mrs. Keller's room—just as Lillian had.

She threw open the door and ran inside. There, on the mirrored dressing table, was an open jewelry box filled with sparkling jewels. Everything was just as it had been in her nightmares. The open balcony doors, the dressing table, the box of jewelry.

Only one thing was different—the man with four fingers wasn't standing over the jewels. He was standing in the doorway, staring at Jessica with a wild look in his eyes.

Slowly, brushing past Jessica, Harry headed for the dressing table. He took his left hand from his pocket and plunged it greedily into the box of jewels.

Jessica felt a sudden jolt of recognition. There it was—the exact scene to complete her nightmare. A four-fingered hand plunged into a pile of glittering jewels.

Suddenly Jessica heard another crack of thunder, much closer and louder than the last one. She bit her lip to keep from crying out in fear.

Harry pulled away from the glittering jewels and turned his gaze on Jessica.

"Lillian's necklace," he whispered.

"*My* necklace," Jessica said shakily.

Harry grinned. "No. You aren't Lillian. I'm afraid I don't believe in ghosts. You're that nosy little girl who's been interviewing Becka Silver."

"No, I'm not," Jessica answered truthfully.

"Oh, but I think you are," Harry said. "And now you're playing detective, aren't you?" He let out a cold, confident laugh. "What did you think? That I was the one who killed Lillian? And that when I saw the necklace again I would panic and suddenly confess?"

Jessica swallowed past a huge lump in her throat. Actually, that was exactly what she'd expected.

Harry laughed again. "Stupid little girl. I didn't kill Lillian."

"I never said you did," Jessica managed to reply. "You're the one who brought it up."

Harry's smile disappeared. "It was Hilda who did it. Just as I've always said—I saw her do it."

Jessica took a deep breath. This was not going the way they had planned. "You're lying," she said. "We . . . I checked. You can't see the balcony from the hallway. Not unless you can see around corners. It's impossible."

Harry turned slowly and looked at the door, then back toward the balcony. "Well, well," he said at last. "So it is."

With a surprisingly quick movement, Harry leaped toward the bedroom door. He closed it quietly, then shoved the deadbolt lock closed.

"Let me out of here!" Jessica cried.

Harry shook his head as he began advancing toward her. "You know, playing detective can be dangerous."

"Stay away from me!" Jessica cried, backing away in terror.

But Harry wasn't listening. "It'll be an amazing story, don't you think? A *second* girl will fall to her death from this same balcony. Naturally, everyone will assume that you were just up here playing around and got careless. And of course, there will be *no* witnesses to your death." He waved his four-fingered hand. "See? Just you and me and a locked door."

"Don't you come near me!" Jessica cried. She found herself backing steadily toward the balcony as Harry kept coming closer, his hands outstretched. This part wasn't in Elizabeth's careful plan. Harry was supposed to have confessed. He wasn't supposed to have locked the door. It had all gone terribly wrong!

"Unicorns!" Jessica cried at the top of her lungs.

Harry paused, staring at her as if she was insane.

"Unicorns!" Jessica cried again.

Elizabeth, Robin, Becka, and Tony raced to the bedroom from the secret two-way mirror where they'd been watching Jessica.

Elizabeth reached it first and grabbed the doorknob, twisting it frantically. It wouldn't budge.

"It's locked!" Elizabeth cried, pushing against the door with her shoulder. "Harry must have locked it from the inside."

Tony tried the door too, without any luck.

"Jessica!" Elizabeth wailed.

"Please, no," Becka said desperately. "We never should have tried this!"

They left Tony trying to break down the heavy door and raced back to their secret observation place in an adjacent room. Members of the crew had cut a hole in the wall behind the dressing table mirror and had replaced the mirror with special glass. A camera was set up there to record everything that happened in the room.

It had been a flawless plan, except for one thing. Harry hadn't panicked. He hadn't confessed. Worst of all, he had locked the door. Elizabeth hadn't planned for any of that. And now Jessica was in terrible danger.

Through the glass, Elizabeth watched in horror as Harry backed Jessica out onto the balcony, his hands outstretched.

*   *   *

"Unicorns?" Harry said, shaking his head. "No, you have it all wrong. Why would Lillian scream *unicorns*? That wouldn't make any sense at all." His eyes glittered madly. "No, what she yelled was *no*. Again and again she yelled it. But first, before we get to that, I'll take that necklace." He moved even closer. "Where did you find it, after all these years?"

"On-on the beach," Jessica stammered. "It washed up on the shore." Jessica clutched at her throat. She knew she should let Harry have the necklace, but for some reason she no longer felt like giving it up. "It's my necklace," she said. "You stay away."

"Your necklace, eh? Not for long."

"Stay away," Jessica cried, her voice shaking.

"That necklace belongs to me," he said. "I'd say I've earned it, wouldn't you? I think Lillian would. If I'd managed to hang on to that necklace, the last fifty years of my life would have been totally different."

"But it's just costume jewelry," Jessica protested. "Glue! I mean, paste!"

Harry laughed out loud. "Some detective. That necklace is worth millions. Millions!" His face went dark again, and he advanced toward her. "I've replayed that moment in my mind for years. That brief moment when I held millions in my hand. All my life I've waited for a chance like that to come again." He laughed. "And what do you know. Here it is."

Jessica felt a cool, damp breeze blowing through her hair and realized with a shock that she had backed all the way out to the edge of the balcony. *Just like Lillian!* she thought frantically. *Just like the dream!*

Suddenly Harry lunged. Jessica jerked back against the railing. A jagged bolt of lightning lit up the sky, and Jessica could see Harry's four-fingered hand reaching for her. She felt a tug around her throat as Harry yanked the necklace from her. "No!" Jessica screamed in anger and terror.

"That's better. That's exactly like Lillian. Only this time, I *won't* drop the necklace. That part will be different," Harry said, "but you'll die just the same! Another terrible accident."

Harry slipped the necklace into his pocket, then seized Jessica by the shoulders.

She felt her shoes slip on the balcony floor.

She felt herself rising in the air, and the railing sliding down her back as Harry lifted her over it. From far away, she heard a frantic pounding noise.

Then she was falling, screaming in sheer terror. Overhead, the dark sky was torn by a bolt of lightning. Below her, Jessica could hear the surf pounding against the jagged rocks. The rocks that had killed Lillian.

Jessica fell, screaming up at the lightning-torn sky.

Then she hit . . . and bounced. And bounced again.

At last she came to rest, lying flat on her back, staring up at the stormy sky.

She took a long, deep breath and shakily climbed to her feet, which wasn't easy to do on the big inflated air bag.

"See?" Will Shipley said as he took Jessica's hand and helped her down onto the rocks, "I told your sister and Becka it would be no problem. What were you screaming for? Nothing to worry about."

Jessica couldn't help laughing with relief. "I don't exactly do this every day, you know. This is my first big acting job."

As Elizabeth and Becka watched through the mirror, Harry took out the necklace and gazed at it, touching the stones and admiring them in the light. He didn't even seem to hear the pounding at the bedroom door as Tony tried to force his way in.

But suddenly he froze, clutching the necklace to his heart. He turned slowly, staring in horror toward the balcony.

"Lillian," he whispered.

"It's the necklace!" Elizabeth said, gripping Becka's hand. "It's affecting him."

"No, Lillian, it can't be," Harry moaned, still staring into thin air.

"She's in there," Elizabeth said in a low whisper. "He can see her!"

"I didn't want to, Lillian," Harry stammered. "I never meant to. I . . . I just wanted the jewels, that's all. I wanted to be rich. Like you."

He paused again, as if he were listening to someone. Then he bowed his head. Slowly he let the necklace fall to the floor. "Yes, I'll tell them. Yes, the time has come."

Just then Tony finally smashed his way through the door and rushed over to take Harry roughly by the arm. Elizabeth, Robin, and Becka raced back to the bedroom, just as Jessica made it to the top of the stairs.

Elizabeth gave Jessica a hug. "You did a great job of acting scared," Elizabeth told her.

Jessica laughed. "Acting, Elizabeth. Just acting."

Seventeen

"You guys ready for your last big scene?" Elizabeth asked as she and Jessica and Robin walked to the Keller mansion for their final day of shooting.

"After last night, I think I may have had it with acting forever," Jessica said. She smiled slyly. "Or at least for a couple of years."

"You were amazing," Elizabeth said.

"So were you. Your plan was perfect." Jessica paused. "Well, almost perfect."

"Becka called last night after you'd gone to sleep. Harry confessed everything to the police," Elizabeth said. "I guess seeing Lillian was too much, even for him. Now I suppose it's up to the police to decide what to do with him."

"It's funny," Robin said. "Even after all the help

Lillian gave us, she was finally the one to catch her killer."

"Lillian is one tough ghost," Jessica said with a smile. "Now that her mission's accomplished, I guess she can rest in peace."

"What about Hilda?" Robin asked. "Has anyone told her?"

"Not yet," Elizabeth said. "But she'll know soon."

"I suppose that cake is wax too," Robin grumbled.

Robin, the twins, and the rest of the extras were gathered around the giant birthday cake for Lillian's party scene.

"Actually," Becka said, "it's a real cake. We had a beautiful artificial cake constructed back at the studio in Hollywood, but while they were driving it here they left it in the back of an unair-conditioned truck." She laughed. "So we ended up with something that looks like a very big melted candle."

"Do we get to eat this real cake?" Jessica asked.

"Not until the scene is totally over, which may never happen if Shawn doesn't join us soon." With a sigh, Becka headed off toward Shawn's dressing room.

A few minutes later they heard Shawn arguing with Becka as the two came onto the set.

"You're rewriting half the movie?" Shawn demanded, glaring angrily at Becka.

"We have no choice," Becka explained. "The

story turns out not to be true. We didn't know the truth until last night."

"Wonderful!" Shawn yelled sarcastically. "So now the Hilda character is practically the star of the whole movie."

"Maybe she'll calm down," Robin said to the twins hopefully. "I really could use a few calm moments before I have to go home to San Diego. This *was* supposed to be a vacation, after all."

But Shawn didn't calm down. Everything was wrong. She didn't like her makeup, she didn't like the new lines of dialogue that had been written for Hilda, and, as usual, she didn't like any of the extras.

When she called Maria a has-been, Jessica gritted her teeth.

When she called Mandy pathetic, Jessica nearly boiled over.

When she called Jessica an airhead again, Jessica was ready to explode.

Finally Shawn turned her anger on Becka. "If you knew how to direct, you idiot, I wouldn't have to go through all this!" Shawn screamed.

Something in Jessica just snapped. She got up very calmly. She walked over to the huge, five-foot-high cake, and dug her hand straight into it.

"Uh-oh," Elizabeth whispered.

"She's not going to do it, is she?" Becka asked.

"I know my sister," Elizabeth said. "She's going to do it."

Jessica threw back her arm and hurled a huge handful of birthday cake through the air. It was a direct hit. The cake landed with a dull splat in the middle of Shawn's forehead.

Shawn's mouth dropped open, and her eyes went wide with rage. But before she could say a word, Mandy walked over to the cake, grabbed her own handful, and let it fly with deadly accuracy.

Seconds later, the rest of the extras joined in, and the air was filled with whizzing gobs of chocolate cake.

Shawn tried to yell, but a piece thrown by Maria muffled her in midshout.

"Excuse me, Becka," Elizabeth said politely. "But I haven't gotten to do much acting, and this looks like a scene I'd really like to be in."

As Elizabeth marched toward the set, she heard one of the camera operators shouting to Becka. "Should I cut?" he asked. "We're still filming!"

"Are you kidding?" Becka shouted back. "Do you know how vain Shawn Brockaway is? With this film, I'll be able to blackmail that rotten little brat for the rest of her life."

"That was truly great," Maria said happily. "I haven't felt that good since we started this movie."

"Have they gotten Shawn cleaned up yet?" Jessica asked.

"That may take a few more hours," Elizabeth replied, licking some icing off her thumb.

Mandy patted Elizabeth on the shoulder. "That was a nice touch when you stuck a big glob down her back."

Elizabeth nodded. "I just hope Becka isn't too mad. Getting that cake here was a lot of work."

The extras turned timidly to where Becka was standing with her assistants, surveying the damage. When Becka saw them she marched over, her face stern. "I just have one thing to say to you ladies," she said grimly.

Jessica stepped forward. "It's all my fault," she confessed "I know I've probably ruined my chances in Hollywood forever, but I just couldn't stand it any longer—"

"Just promise me one thing," Becka said, holding up a warning finger.

"Anything," Jessica vowed.

Becka broke into a wide grin. "When you come to the premiere party for the movie next year, promise me you won't go anywhere *near* the cake!"

"Premiere party?" Jessica echoed. She turned to Mandy and Maria. "Wait'll the Unicorns hear about *this!*"

"Jessica! Robin!" Elizabeth whispered, pulling them aside.

"Hang on. Mandy and I were just deciding what to wear to the premiere," Jessica protested.

"Look!" Elizabeth pointed across the room to an old woman standing uncertainly in the doorway.

"Hilda?" Jessica gave her sister a puzzled look.

"I called her and asked her to come," Elizabeth said. "You'll understand in a minute."

Elizabeth and the girls greeted Hilda and took her to the screening room. Becka had arranged for a film to be shot of the set with no one on it. The film was already loaded into the projector.

"Mrs. Zalanski, we have something that belongs to you," Elizabeth told the old woman. She reached into her pocket and pulled out a tissue-wrapped bundle. It was strange, but she no longer felt any attraction to the necklace. She handed it to Hilda.

"Oh, my goodness," Hilda said softly.

"It's yours now," Jessica said. She grinned. "I can't believe we've been carrying around a million-dollar necklace in our backpacks."

"Your name's been cleared," Robin added gently. "Harry killed Lillian. And now he's confessed to the police."

"But how—?" Hilda began in confusion.

"We have a feeling there's someone who will be able to explain everything better than we can," Elizabeth said. She led Hilda to a seat, while Jessica turned out the lights.

"A movie?" Hilda asked, clutching the necklace to her chest.

"Yes," Elizabeth said. "A special movie, just for you." She flicked on the projector.

There, on the screen, was the ballroom set. For a

few moments, that was all. Hilda looked over at Elizabeth, a question in her eyes.

"Wait," Elizabeth said.

While they all watched silently, a young girl slowly materialized on the screen. Her face was pale, but on her lips there was a hint of a smile.

"Lillian!" Hilda whispered.

"I can see her a little now," Jessica told Elizabeth and Robin.

"I can't see her at all," Robin said.

"Yes, Lillian, I can hear you," Hilda said, speaking to the screen. "Yes, I understand, Lillian. I understand it all."

"She can hear her!" Robin whispered.

"I think we should leave them alone," Jessica said suddenly. "They probably have a lot to talk about."